ROBIN ON HIS OWN

ROBIN ON HIS OWN

Johnniece Marshall Wilson

SCHOLASTIC
HARDCOVER

Scholastic Inc.
New York

Library of Congress Cataloging-in-Publication Data

Wilson, Johnniece Marshall.
  Robin on his own / Johnniece Marshall Wilson.
    p.   cm.
  Summary: A black boy whose family is in transition tries to come to
terms with the death of his mother.
  ISBN 0-590-41813-0

  [1. Death — Fiction. 2. Mothers and sons — Fiction. 3. Afro-
Americans — Fiction.] I. Title.
PZ7.W696514Ro   1990
[Fic] — dc20   90-32927
                                                               CIP
                                                                AC

12 11 10 9 8 7 6 5 4 3 2 1   0 1 2 3 4 5/9
Printed in the U.S.A.   37
First Scholastic printing, October 1990

*To my children —
Karin, Natalie, and Tonya*

One

WATUSI was mewing. At first, it'd been soft; now it was loud, desperate. Robin usually got up early on Saturday mornings to watch cartoons, but that day he'd been tired and had slept in — until Watusi began mewing so loud, Robin heard him all the way up to the second floor.

He threw aside the covers, sat up, and pulled on his robe. He didn't bother with his slippers. He wanted to get downstairs fast so Watusi wouldn't wake his father or Aunt Belle.

Moving out into the hallway, Robin walked carefully past the guest room, where his Aunt Belle stayed. She'd moved in a few days before Robin's mother's illness had gotten worse. And she'd been there ever since. He walked past

1

the weak spot in the floor at the top of the landing. If he stepped on it in the quiet house, the sound would be as loud as a cherry bomb exploding, and sure to wake his father, who had stayed up late rewriting some music he wanted to perform that weekend.

The carpets on the stairs were so thick, he almost slipped and fell. He grabbed the banister, held on, and made his way quietly and safely down the stairs. He went through the living room and dining room, and out through the kitchen to the sun porch.

Watusi always slept out on the sun porch. But Watusi wasn't there now. Robin opened the outside door and looked out. As soon as he'd opened the door, he saw his cat. Watusi's orange and black tortoiseshell fur glistened with morning dew. Watusi was standing on his hind-paws, clawing at the screen door.

"Oh, Watusi," Robin said. Watusi looked in at Robin and clawed harder at the screen door. "Don't tell me I left you outdoors all night."

Robin unhooked the screen door and pushed gently against it. Watusi crouched on the top step. Robin opened the door wider and Watusi leapt inside. He jumped up and clawed at Robin's terry cloth robe. Then Watusi rubbed against Robin's leg. Robin patted Watusi's head. "I bet you're hungry after being out all night."

After he'd fed Watusi and put fresh water

into the dish, Robin went into the living room. Might as well watch cartoons, he thought. He was no longer sleepy. Anyway, it was too hot to go back to bed. He went back to latch the screen door on the sun porch when he heard, "PSST!"

Robin opened the door just wide enough to get his head through. He looked around. He didn't see anyone.

He started to close the door and latch it when he spotted his best friend, Benny, out near the tall, unclipped hedges. He'd have to remember to clip the hedges before his aunt got married. She wanted to have the reception in their backyard, weather permitting.

He looked at the hedges again. Benny was scrunched low, his hair just visible over the top of the hedges. Where leaves did not grow thick, Robin could make out Benny's plaid shirt. Benny loved plaid shirts and always wore them.

"Benny? Hey, Benny!" Robin yelled. "What are you doing out there so early?"

Benny straightened up. He was lots taller than the hedges, two heads taller than Robin. Robin was short and stocky. Benny was tall and thin. "Let's play kickball," said Benny. "I got a new one." He held the shiny ball up, then set it on top of the hedges.

"It's neat," Robin said. "Come on into the yard."

There was no gate, just a large split in the hedges.

Benny picked the ball up and came through. "You can't play like that, Shorty," Benny said.

Robin looked at his pajamas. His robe hung open. Threads dangled loose and frayed where Watusi'd pulled at it. He wiggled his bare toes up and down. "I'll go change."

Benny grabbed Robin's arm. "We can't play kickball alone. Where is everybody?"

"Probably still at home in bed," Robin said. "Or watching cartoons."

"They promised," Benny said. "We made a pact."

"When we made the pact, I bet you we weren't talking 'bout five o'clock in the morning," Robin said, and laughed.

"It must be almost eight o'clock," Benny told him. He started bouncing the ball on the concrete walkway. "We said we'd play every Saturday, all summer." Benny bounced the ball some more. "Sure wish my yard was this big. We could've been playing over there."

"It probably seems like daybreak to everyone," Robin said. "Maybe they'll show up later. They won't forget." But he had forgotten. He had had other things on his mind, like his father going off more and more to make music. And now his aunt had suddenly announced that she was going to get married.

4

But at least the thought that usually occupied his mind hadn't come today. He hadn't thought about his mother yet. How much he missed her. How he dreamed about her almost every night.

So far, he'd been able to keep the kickball pact all right. This was the beginning of August and this was the first Saturday he'd forgotten. He didn't want to forget again. Maybe he wouldn't think about other things if he spent more time playing kickball.

Robin started inside. Over his shoulder he said, "Come in and call the gang if you wanna."

Benny bounced the ball. "Okay," he said. "But I hope they're already on the way over."

"Call Cyndy," Robin said. "I bet you she's up. She knows everything that's going on 'round here. She *has* to get up early."

Benny followed Robin into the sun porch. He flung the ball into a corner and startled Watusi. The cat leapt aside, then went back to his food dish.

"Be quiet! My father and my aunt are still asleep," Robin said. He went upstairs to get dressed.

Benny got the telephone off the dining room table and carried it into the living room. He sprawled out in a corner of the sofa. He lifted the receiver and started dialing.

Two

In his room, Robin was trying to decide which shirt to put on. Without wanting to, he thought about his mother. Maybe it was the drawer full of shirts that did it. She'd wanted him to keep his shirts folded perfectly. And they were, after all these months.

He'd opened the drawer, and the lilac polo shirt she'd loved so much was on top. He almost touched it but caught himself in time. He had worn it to school under his jacket the day she died. He wasn't ready yet to wear it again.

Robin closed the drawer and looked across to his mother's picture on the bureau. The picture was in a double frame. One side was an eight-by-ten glossy of his mother by herself. The other side of the frame held a matte-finished picture of the three of them together. Charles Lazarus, his father, grinned back at him. His mother'd been smiling, too. He hadn't smiled. He stared sleepily into the camera. A little while after the picture'd been taken, she'd started to get sick. It seemed like yesterday.

Robin looked down. The shirt drawer was still open. He slammed it shut with his knee. He opened another drawer and took out a short-sleeved navy blue sweatshirt. He closed the drawer and slipped the shirt on. He straightened the creases in his jeans and went downstairs carrying his gym shoes.

When he got downstairs, Benny was in the living room playing with Watusi. Watusi was standing on the sofa cushion, his back arched, hissing at Benny.

"You better stop teasing Watusi. He's gonna scratch you," Robin said, crossing to the sofa. He sat down and started putting on his shoes.

"Watusi won't do that. He knows I'm his friend," Benny said. He curled his fingers as if they were claws and motioned at Watusi.

"All right. If he scratches you, don't say I didn't warn you." Robin finished tying his shoe-laces.

Benny hopped up. "You ready?"

Robin looked at his friend. "Did you ever live on a farm?"

Benny shook his head. "Why do you ask?"

"I don't know. I guess 'cause you get up so early. Even earlier than me."

"It's my folks' fault. Mama gets up and starts blasting her radio at the crack of dawn. Who can sleep?"

"Do you know I didn't eat breakfast?"

"Me, neither," Benny said. He moved toward the kitchen. "What kinda cold cereal you got?"

"I don't know. Let's see."

They went into the kitchen. The old-fashioned refrigerator in the corner hummed and clicked on. At first it was just the whir of an engine; then it popped, roared, and clanged like it was falling apart.

Benny stared at the fridge. "What's wrong with your refrigerator?"

"It's just old, I guess," Robin told him. Looking in the pantry, he said, "Which do you like, oats or bran?"

Benny stuck his tongue out and said, "Yuk! Bring on the oats."

They ate cold cereal shaped like toy cars. The fridge clicked off. The kitchen was silent.

After a time Benny said, "The gang should be here soon. I called everybody. When I called Cyndy, she said she was just getting ready to call you."

"Told you she'd be up."

"With my new ball, we oughta have a real

interesting game. You wanna play girls against boys?'' Benny went right on talking between spoonfuls of cereal, but Robin seemed far away.

"Are you listening to me, Robin?''

Robin nodded and finished his cereal. Suddenly he didn't feel like playing kickball anymore, but if the gang was coming, he'd have to do something. He pushed back his chair and got up. He put his bowl and spoon into the sink and filled it with water. He squirted in a few drops of detergent.

After he'd washed, dried, and put away the dishes, he heard the gang out in the backyard.

"Hey! Shorty, come on out!'' That was Cyndy. She lived in the big redbrick house on the corner. Naturally, Robin thought, she'd show up first.

Robin and Benny went outside.

They chose up sides. Benny picked one team — Robin, the other. They didn't play boys against girls after all. When Benny suggested it, Cyndy shook her head. Her ponytail flying, she said, "No, Benjamin, that's sexist. We want a coed team. Or else I won't play. None of the girls will play.'' She looked at the other girls. They stared at her. "Isn't that right?'' The other girls nodded.

"Then you can go home,'' Benny told her. "Besides, my name's Benedict.''

Cyndy ignored that. She stamped her foot.

"No. I won't go home unless Robin tells me to. It's his yard. Don't be so bossy."

"B-B-B-B-Bossy?!" Benny sputtered. He closed his mouth and turned to look at Robin.

Robin was standing a little way off from the group. He had heard everything. But he thought that Cyndy watched too much TV. He said nothing. His interest in playing kickball was fading away more and more as he listened to the gang bicker among themselves.

"We'd better get this game started. Pretty soon it'll be lunchtime," Cyndy said.

Softly, Benny muttered, "Look how bossy she is. And she's calling *me* bossy." Louder, he said, "I pick the twins."

Walking side by side, the twins marched across the yard and stood behind Benny.

The kids were quiet in the yard. The only sound was cars moving along the street. It was a dead-end street and there was seldom a lot of traffic. It was Robin's turn to pick. He stood still, idly, as if he didn't realize anything was going on around him.

"Are you going to pick somebody?" Cyndy asked. "Or go on standing there like a statue?"

Robin still didn't move. Benny said, "Robin, please pick somebody."

Without thinking about it, Robin said, "Cyndy . . ."

Cyndy tilted her head. Her ponytail flew. She

grinned at the gang and went and stood behind Robin.

Benny said, "I pick Bobby."

Bobby stood behind Benny.

Robin saw that it was his turn again. He was more alert this time. "Rick . . . "

After team members had been selected, Robin looked over his team and wished he hadn't been thinking about anything else. They couldn't possibly win the game now. For one thing, he hadn't meant to choose Cyndy. Not right off like that. It wasn't that she couldn't play. She was a very good player, but she was too bossy. He probably would've ended up with her anyway, but still, if he had been paying attention, he could've watched her get nervous. She always got nervous when she was chosen last. Now they'd have to take turns marking scores on the walkway with a piece of chalk. There was an even number of players so that he and Benny had the same amount. Sometimes if there was an odd player, that person would keep score and referee.

As Robin moved with his team members to their end of the yard, he saw that Cyndy was already giving orders to the others.

"Come on, guys. Let's go get 'em!" she yelled.

"Oh, brother," Robin mumbled.

When they were at the opposite end of the yard, Cyndy hollered, "Play ball."

For about fifteen minutes, they played a really dull game. One time, Robin kicked the ball too hard. It flew into the air and landed on the top of the neighbor's garage. They thought it was stuck there, but it rolled off on the other side. Robin went to get it. It was declared foul, but when he kicked the ball a second time, it lodged itself between the branches in the hedges at the other end of the yard. Since it was Benny's territory, he went and got it himself.

"That's the last time I'll let you guys play with my new ball," Benny called. He spent a long time checking the ball for scratches.

By the time Benny got back into the yard, nobody wanted to finish the game. They were all sitting on the steps, filling them as if they were seated on bleachers watching a game. Watusi sat on the concrete walk and watched them. Bobby Knuckles, who lived next door, broke off a long blade of grass and teased Watusi with it.

But even Watusi didn't feel like playing. He stayed rooted on the walkway and poked a white-tipped paw at the blade of grass. After a while, Bobby threw the blade of grass away.

Benny stood on the walk. He twirled the ball around and around on his fingertips. "Well, are we gonna play or not?"

No one said anything. Not even Cyndy, although she had a point of view about everything.

On the steps there was a little bit of space between the twins and Robin. Benny tossed the ball onto the lawn and squeezed into the space between Robin and the twins. Together the twins scooted over a little and made a space for him.

"It must be this heat," Robin said finally.

"It's not that hot," Benny told him. "Maybe you need to take off that sweater."

"It ain't a sweater. It's a sweatshirt."

"That's even worse," Benny said.

"You can't talk. You got on a long-sleeved shirt. All the heat in the world must be getting caught in that plaid."

They were silent again. From the walkway, Watusi stared up at them.

Roy Butler stood and stretched. "I'm going home," he said. "Maybe I'll catch the rest of the cartoons." He went down the walk and through the break in the hedges. " 'Bye," he said, as he turned and waved and moved up the sidewalk.

Cyndy rose. "My mother usually lets me help her bake cookies along about now." She waved as she went through the break in the hedges.

Benny got up and retrieved the ball from the grass. Coming back to the steps, he bounced the ball on the walkway. Between bounces, he said, "Maybe my father'll take me fishing." Still bouncing the ball, he left, too.

Soon they had all left. Robin stood on the

steps. Although he couldn't see Benny, he could still hear the ball bouncing on the sidewalk.

After they left, Robin stayed on the steps. He sat with his back pressed against the screen door. He knew that if he sat quietly there, he'd think about his mother again, but he was too tired to try to find anything else to do, so he stayed, pressed against the screen door.

Three

Now that he was sitting still, it was cooler in the backyard. A breeze stirred the leaves in the two big trees at the far end of the yard. It hadn't been too hot to play kickball at all. Robin realized that everyone had simply lost interest in the game. He hoped it wasn't going to be like that for the rest of the summer. He closed his eyes.

And the thoughts came. Like always, he remembered the bad parts. The bad parts that he didn't want to remember. He wanted to hold in his mind the thoughts of his mother the way she was on the days before she started getting sick.

Mr. Lazarus hadn't let Robin go to the burial.

15

Robin had gone to the church for the services that Friday, but Tex and Raimi had sat in the car with him outside the cemetery until it was all over.

Robin opened his eyes. Watusi climbed the steps and lay down at Robin's side and went to sleep. He stroked Watusi's fur and sat listening for his Aunt Belle.

A few minutes later, he heard her come downstairs. He knew she was dressed to go out. It was something in the way her high-heeled shoes caught on the carpet. He knew she was moving toward the back of the house, to the kitchen. He heard the floors creak in the old house as his aunt strode across the tiled kitchen floor.

" 'Morning, Robin," Aunt Belle said.

"Good morning, Aunt Belle." He hopped off the steps so fast, he almost knocked Watusi over. "Oops! Come on," he said to Watusi. Robin jerked the door open. Cat and boy leapt inside.

"You two sure have a lot of energy this morning," Aunt Belle said.

He gazed at his aunt as she stood in the sun porch. She looked beautiful, Robin thought. Her white dress caught the sunlight and almost blinded him. He knew she liked to wear white in summer. It kept her cool, or so she'd told him.

"I guess Monroe didn't get here yet."

"Not yet," Robin told her. He continued to stare. Watusi had curled up into a ball in a corner of the sun porch and gone back to sleep.

"I'll make you breakfast," she said, going back into the kitchen.

"Benny and I made cold cereal before the kickball game."

"Kickball game? Already? How long have you been up?"

Robin hadn't noticed the time. "Early," he said.

"I forgot. You like to get up early. You're Tracy's boy, all right."

Nervously, Robin rubbed his eyes. He opened his mouth to say something, then closed it again. Aunt Belle had said his mother's name. He remembered he hadn't even seen her headstone. All sorts of thoughts started colliding in his head: his mother's death, not getting to tell her good-bye, Aunt Belle getting married, his father going off to make music with his jazz band. He felt dizzy.

"Are you sure you're not hungry?" his aunt said.

Robin shook his head. He listened to his Aunt Belle make a pot of coffee for his father, who liked fresh coffee first thing. Robin got up and went into the living room. He turned on the TV and slumped down onto the sofa.

He had already seen the cartoons, but he was too tired to change channels. He stayed on the sofa. From where he sat, he had only to turn his head and look out the screen door. He sat there staring. From the corner of his eye, he caught a movement on the sidewalk. He pulled himself up, leaned forward, and looked out the door. There was a man standing on the sidewalk. He'd stopped in front of their house, then turned in through the gate. The man held a small container in one hand. In the other was a piece of paper. Robin noticed that the man's hands were so big that the piece of paper was almost hidden in it. The man moved slowly up the walk toward the house. Before he got to the porch, he stopped to look at the piece of paper again.

When the man climbed up onto the porch, he stuck the piece of paper into the pocket of his blue-flowered shirt. He rapped softly on the screen door.

Robin didn't move. From the kitchen, Aunt Belle said, "That'll be Monroe. Get that, will you?"

Without answering, Robin got up and inched his way to the door.

Monroe rapped again.

Aunt Belle said, "Robin?"

Finally Robin unlatched the screen door and pushed it open. The man stood on the porch, filling the doorway. Robin gaped at him, then remembered it wasn't polite to stare. He looked at the covered container. He could hear faint scratching sounds coming from it. Robin stared, fascinated.

The man leaned down until he was eye level with Robin. "Hello, young fella," he said. "I'm looking for Miss Belle Lazarus." The man grinned, showing big, perfect white teeth. Like some kind of monster, Robin thought. "I'm Monroe Morrison. Call me Monroe."

"Come in," Robin said. He opened the door wider. Monroe straightened up again and, head bent, stepped inside. Then, Robin yelled, "Aunt Belle . . ."

In the living room, Monroe set the container in a corner near the lamp table. He stood in the doorway until Aunt Belle came in. He had removed his straw hat. He fanned himself with it. Robin saw that Monroe's head was bald. Monroe mopped his head with a wadded handkerchief. Looks like a giant brown egg, Robin thought. He noticed that Monroe more than made up for the lack of hair on his head because he sported the longest, shaggiest beard Robin had ever seen.

Wiping her hands on an apron, Aunt Belle came out of the kitchen.

"Oh, how are you, Monroe?" She grinned up at him. Aunt Belle was tall, but Robin saw that this Monroe Morrison towered over her.

19

Robin had gone back to the corner of the sofa and slumped down. He watched as Monroe kissed Aunt Belle. She took his hat and put it on the end table.

"You look great, Belle," Monroe said. "Tell me, is it always this hot 'round here?"

"Hot? Man, we're having a cold wave. You should've been here yesterday. But they do say this is the hottest summer on record." She moved to the big chair under the picture window. "Sit down, put your feet up. Relax. I'll get you some orange juice." She went into the kitchen.

She returned, carrying two glasses of juice. She gave one to Monroe and the other to Robin. She sat on the opposite end of the sofa. Robin stayed in his corner, sipping juice and staring at the TV as if he were interested in the cartoons. What really held his attention were the scratching sounds coming from the covered container in the corner. The sounds reminded Robin of mice. His friend Cyndy had white mice for pets. He'd heard them scratch around in their cage lots of times.

"This is my favorite nephew I was telling you about. Isn't he sweet?"

"Hee hee hee," Monroe laughed, and flashed his big teeth again. "He sure is."

Robin smiled and looked away. He'd only taken his eyes off the container for a moment. Monroe leapt up, set his glass on a coaster on the coffee table, and grabbed the container. "I brought this for you, son." He handed the container to Robin.

"Me?" Robin stared at the container. It was square. The cover reminded Robin of the cover his mother used to put over the toaster. While he stared, the scratching sounds grew louder. It sounded like two mice now. Monroe stood in front of him holding the container. Reluctantly Robin took it. He set it on the coffee table.

He stared at the container a few seconds. Then he stared at the TV. On TV, Wile E. Coyote was trying to catch the Roadrunner. Robin stopped looking. He'd already seen the cartoon. He knew how it'd come out. He stole a glance at Aunt Belle. And at her friend Monroe. Again Robin heard something in the container scratching like it wanted to get out. Monroe and Aunt Belle were waiting for him to uncover the container.

Robin eyed it again. Every once in a while the scratching came faster. He looked at his aunt and at Monroe. Monroe sipped orange juice. Aunt Belle simply sat on the end of the sofa, waiting.

The scratching continued. Robin lifted the cover off the container and let it fall to the floor.

Four

ROBIN stared into the bird cage. Inside was the most beautiful parakeet in the world. The parakeet was pale yellow with a tiny bit of orange and blue on its wings. Robin didn't know what to say. The TV blared in the background. Nobody bothered to watch it. Robin stared at the parakeet. No wonder, he thought, there was so much scratching.

Out of the corner of his eye he saw that Aunt Belle and Monroe were watching him. Aunt Belle wanted him to say something. Anything. But he kept on gazing into the cage.

"Thanks, Monroe," he said finally, and without looking away from the bird cage. The parakeet walked along the bottom of the cage, eating birdseed that had fallen out of the dish that hung on the side of the cage.

"You're welcome," Monroe told him. "You got a name for her?"

"Polly — Pollymae," Robin said.

"Belle told me how much you like animals. Next time I come by, I hope you'll have taught Pollymae to talk." Monroe tugged at his beard.

"Talk? Will that take long?"

"Sometimes. Sometimes they learn right away. She can already sing like a dream. She sings as sweet as Belle does. Do you sing, Robin?"

Robin was still peering into the cage. He looked up. "I used to sing in the choir at church. At school, too. I always sang in church when — " He'd almost said, "When my mother was here." Instead he said, "I still sing in the children's choir when I go to church."

Monroe was about to say something else when Mr. Lazarus came downstairs carrying a small overnight bag. He crossed the room and set the bag near the door.

With a long brown finger, Aunt Belle pointed to the bag. "I see you're off and running again. You will be available for my wedding, won't you?"

"Got to make some extra money," Mr. Lazarus said.

Monroe stood up. Aunt Belle said, "This is Monroe. Monroe, this is my brother, Charles Lazarus."

They shook hands. Monroe said, "Pleased to meet you."

"Likewise," Mr. Lazarus said, and released Monroe's hand. "That's some grip." He grinned and flexed his fingers.

"I used to be a boxer. Or thought I was. Then I realized these hands should be put to more delicate use," Monroe said, and sat down again.

Aunt Belle said, "Monroe has his own appliance repair business."

Mr. Lazarus nodded.

Monroe crossed his legs. His knobby knees almost reached his chin. He drew a container of fat brown cigars from his pocket. He shook them to the top and offered one to Mr. Lazarus.

"No thanks," Mr. Lazarus said. He turned to Robin, who was still staring at the parakeet. "Well, well," he said to Robin, and looked into the parakeet cage. He pulled a hassock closer to the coffee table and sat down.

Robin had poked his finger into the cage. Pollymae lit on it as if it were a perch. It tickled.

"Did you give it a name yet?" his father asked.

"Yes. I'm gonna call her Pollymae."

Mr. Lazarus nodded at his son.

They were silent for a time. Pollymae hopped

24

down and scratched around in the cage. Then the refrigerator clicked on and roared to life. The noise seemed to get louder each time it clicked on. It clanged and roared and whirred like it was about to blow a gasket, if it hadn't already.

"Sounds like that refrigerator could stand a repair job," Aunt Belle said, and turned to Monroe. "Looks like I brought you to the right place."

Suddenly the refrigerator popped and screeched. "And in the nick of time," Mr. Lazarus said. "I've been meaning to have somebody look at that."

"I'll get some coffee," Aunt Belle said, standing. She went into the kitchen.

When she returned with the coffee, she said, "You know, I think Robin looks more like Tracy, don't you, Charles?"

She poured the coffee and served it all around.

"Yes. He does." Robin heard his father agree with his aunt. He thought about how his mother would give him very weak cups of coffee, more cream than anything else. And it seemed strange to hear them talk about her like that. Especially since he could hardly think about anybody else.

Mr. Lazarus sipped his coffee, set his cup down, and said, "Okay, so when's the wedding? I've got to make sure I'm in town."

"You'd better be," Aunt Belle said.

25

"It's the last Saturday in August," Monroe said.

Out on the sun porch Watusi woke up and came back into the living room. He stood and arched his back. When he got to the bird cage, he stared at Pollymae, then hopped up onto the sofa. Watusi flipped over and lay down. Soon he was sound asleep again.

"I can never get over how much your cat acts like a human being," Aunt Belle said to Robin.

Robin looked up but said nothing.

"I'll bet Robin treats him like a human being, too," Monroe said.

Before they could finish their coffee, there was a blast from a horn. The blast sounded rhythmic, like a song. Tires squealed along the street. Craning his neck and looking through the living room window, Robin saw the van pull into their driveway. Once parked, the driver tooted the horn a couple of times more, for good measure.

Aunt Belle frowned. "That's Charles's group," she said to Monroe.

Robin hopped up so fast, he scared Pollymae. She skittered around in the cage. Her feathers flew. She went to roost on the perch.

Aunt Belle got up and pulled Monroe up with her. "Come on. You might as well meet them, too. They're like family around here."

They went out onto the porch. The screen door slapped shut behind them.

Left alone on the sofa, Watusi flipped over again but didn't wake up. In his sleep he stretched again, as if he were grateful that he finally had the sofa to himself.

In the bird cage on the coffee table, Pollymae sang softly as she swung to and fro on her perch.

Five

LEANING over the brick banister, Robin watched as Raimi, Tex, Luther, and Buddy climbed out of the van. They went around to the back of the van and opened the rear door to get their instruments. Robin held the screen door so they could go inside.

"Hey there, Robin," Tex said as he bounded up the steps. He had his guitar case in his right hand. With his free hand he took off his cowboy hat and fanned Robin with it. "You still singing in the choir? I bet you'll sing with us soon, huh?"

Robin shook his head, then said, "I've got a parakeet. She might sing with you."

"We'll have to give her a listen." Tex started

into the house. He stopped, turned, and gestured at Robin with the cowboy hat. "Does she talk?"

"Not yet. Monroe says I can teach her."

"If you put a hood over the cage and peep under it while you're teaching her, she'll learn faster," Tex told him.

"I'll try that, then." Robin held the door, and Tex went inside the house and down into the cellar.

The other bandsmen came up onto the porch and followed Tex down to the cellar. Raimi was last. But then, he had the bulkier equipment. He carried his drums, all of them fitted one inside the other. He was the shortest player and had the largest instrument. He struggled up onto the porch with the drums as if they weighed a ton. The drumsticks were sticking out of his back pocket. The drums were silver and gleamed in the midday sun. Robin had to look away from them.

"Let me help you with that," Monroe said to Raimi. Monroe got off the banister, where he'd been sitting next to Aunt Belle, and grabbed part of the drum set.

Robin held the door until everyone had gone inside, then he let the screen door slam shut. He stopped in the living room. Watusi shuddered in his sleep on the sofa when the screen door slammed. Pollymae never stopped singing.

Robin went down to the cellar to listen to the band rehearse.

In the cellar the bandsmen were getting their instruments ready.

As he moved down the stairs, Robin heard Monroe say, "I think you better fix this. I don't know anything about music except how to turn on a stereo." He could see that they were trying to place the drums on their little stands.

Standing off to one side, Luther twiddled with the leather strap that he used to hold his saxophone. Whether he was playing the sax or not, he always wore the leather strap around his neck. Even in church. Robin remembered seeing Luther fiddle with the strap when Luther should've been singing the hymns along with everyone else.

After the instruments had all been set up, the band started playing. They jammed for one solid hour before taking a break. This time they had an audience. Monroe, Aunt Belle, and Robin stayed downstairs to listen. Even Watusi had come downstairs to listen. He had curled himself into a ball on the cool wood of the cellar steps.

When they took a breather, Mr. Lazarus went upstairs and got a pitcher of lemonade and some glasses. He served lemonade in tall frosty glasses all around.

Robin poured a tiny bit of lemonade into a

coaster for Watusi. Watusi lapped it up, then immediately went back to sleep.

When thirsts had been quenched, the band started jamming again.

Sitting on the steps, leaning against the wall, Robin listened. Aunt Belle and Monroe sat at the corner bar and kept time with the music. Robin heard Monroe say, "They're good. Real good." Monroe's big teeth flashed. His bald head gleamed in the light.

They must have an important job, Robin thought. He wondered how much longer this could last. The basement jam sessions; all of them together. With Aunt Belle getting married and moving to Monroe's hometown, Wheeling, West Virginia, not only would he not see them, but things would never be the same again.

Less than an hour later, the band stopped jamming. It was time to go.

Mr. Lazarus said, "Well, load up, fellas. We've got a ways to travel. Robin, help me with these glasses."

Robin got off the steps and went upstairs carrying the pitcher. Watusi raced upstairs ahead of him.

Upstairs, what his father really wanted was to give Robin even worse bad news. They were in the kitchen. Mr. Lazarus was stacking glasses in the sink.

"I'm selling the house, Robin," his father said as he filled the sink with water. "It's time to start packing up your things."

Robin said nothing.

His father went on. "This house'll be too big for the two of us."

A beat of time passed. Water rushed into the sink and spattered the counter.

"It is pretty big," Robin said, finally. "But I like lots of space." He thought about their big backyard. No more kickball games. "Will you get a smaller house?"

"No. I was thinking more about an apartment."

No pets, either, Robin thought. He was going to mention Watusi and Pollymae, but his father had finished the glasses and set them to dry.

"I've got to go," Mr. Lazarus said, wiping his hands on a paper towel. He tossed it into the garbage.

From outside they heard a car horn.

In the living room Mr. Lazarus grabbed his bag. Turning to face Robin, he said, "You be good. Mind your aunt. Okay?"

Mr. Lazarus went out the door. Through the screen he said, "I'll only be gone tonight and tomorrow."

Robin was still thinking about what his father had said. It gnawed at him so much, he almost didn't say, "Have a good time, Daddy." He was thinking about the apartment. Maybe he hadn't heard right. After all, Pollymae had been singing in the background. Water had been pouring into the sink; the band members had been clattering around with their instruments. And he had been thinking about Aunt Belle's wedding. He would just have to wait until Sunday night to ask his father.

Robin went out onto the porch and watched his father climb into the van, just like he always did. Raimi was driving. He threw the van into gear, and they roared away.

Aunt Belle came outside and stood on the porch, clasping her hands. Robin sat on the steps and watched as the van disappeared up the street and around the corner.

When he could no longer see the van, Robin stared at the verbena his mother had planted last summer. The small red flowers looked good in the grass and against the dark green leaves of the plant itself.

Aunt Belle said, "Let's work on the list, Monroe. Robin, you coming along?"

"Maybe later," Robin said. He didn't move. Aunt Belle opened the screen door. Watusi streaked outside. He sat on Robin's lap. Robin stroked Watusi's fur. The last thing Robin wanted to do was work on the list. So he sat on the steps, Watusi cradled in his lap, and looked at the flowers.

Six

ROBIN went on staring at the flower beds his mother had planted so long ago. Only it didn't seem like a long time anymore. Whenever a breeze came up, he could smell their fragrance. His mother had had a green thumb, and the yard looked like splotches of his watercolors on a green background. He pushed Watusi off his lap and leaned over. He rested his elbows on his knees, his chin in his hands. He had sat this way a long time when the thought came to him: Where was the band going to practice? Had his father even thought of that? Robin tried to picture the band practicing in the cramped living room of an apartment. He couldn't. He could barely picture their piano in an apartment, or what an apartment looked like. The only person he knew who'd lived in an apartment was Aunt Belle. She'd had a little studio across town near the high school, where she taught music. All his friends lived in one-family houses. In his neighborhood.

While Robin was still on the steps, Monroe came out. He clutched his big straw hat by the brim. "Well, I'll be going, young man," Monroe said. "I've helped Belle with the list as much as I could. Now it's your turn." Monroe grinned. Robin tried to smile, but he couldn't get his mouth to cooperate.

Monroe put his hat on and started down the walkway. "Oh, I hope you'll have fun with your parakeet. You promise me you'll really try to teach Pollymae how to talk?"

"Yes. Yes, I will," Robin said. "Thanks for getting her for me."

Monroe smoothed his beard and went down the walk.

"So, you've decided to help me out here?" Aunt Belle asked. "You stayed out there so long, makes me think you don't really want me to get married."

"I do want you to get married," Robin said, but he didn't sound convincing even to his own ears. He slumped onto the sofa.

"I've waited a long time and I want to get

this right." Aunt Belle had spread out on the coffee table notebooks and sheets of paper where she'd made her lists. Robin noticed she'd scratched out some names, only to write them in again.

His back pressed against the sofa, he thought about how his mother had loved their old house, too. He thought how one Friday she'd made him help her hang curtains in the kitchen. He knew it was a Friday. It had been the last day of school and he was looking forward to playing in the backyard, but she'd come home with new curtains and had said she needed his help.

The curtains were still there. Aunt Belle had taken them down to be washed every once in a while, but the fruit and vegetable pattern on a gold background was just as bright and clear as it'd been on the day the curtains were hung. His father still hadn't fixed the curtain rod. It was a little askew, just as it had been when Robin stood on the sink and held one end while his mother nailed it up.

He knew they could take the curtains if they moved, but it wouldn't be the same. The thing was, he didn't want to move. He'd never lived anywhere else. And he didn't *want* to live anywhere else.

Robin felt his eyes getting full, and he blinked back the tears. He felt even more abandoned than he'd felt when Aunt Belle had announced that she was getting married.

"You're awfully quiet," Aunt Belle said.

"I'm all right." He sniffled and sat up.

"Did you feed and water Pollymae?"

"Yes," Robin said. He had already moved the cage to the sun porch. He'd hung the cage on a hook out there where his mother used to hang freshly ironed clothes until she could put them into their proper closets. It had turned out to be the perfect spot for a bird cage. Pollymae sang softly. Robin could hear the perch in the cage creaking as the parakeet swung back and forth. He got up, crossed the room, and turned on the TV. It was too early for any good shows, but he felt like watching TV. So he did.

Seven

HE went back to the sofa and slumped down.
With Aunt Belle riffling papers at his side, he
grew restless and would not sit still. He saw
how excited she was about getting married. And
all he did was want things to stay the same. He
got up again and went into the kitchen. The
refrigerator clicked on, hummed, roared, popped,
trembled, rattled, and shook the house. Robin
stared at it as if he were willing it to be quiet.
It did no such thing. If anything, it clanged
louder until it was through.

From the living room, Aunt Belle said, "Bring
out the cookies. I could eat one myself." He
realized it was the first time he'd sampled the
cookies she'd baked the night before. And they

were his favorite — chocolate chip. Robin brought the cookies.

He set the cookie jar on the coffee table, took another cookie, and nestled into a corner of the sofa. "What're all these papers? All that can't be the guest list," he said.

"I'm afraid it is," Aunt Belle said. She uncapped her fountain pen and scribbled something into a notebook. "I'm trying to pare it down to a smaller size. You know, everybody ought to get married as young as possible. When you wait until you're my age, you've met too many people. I don't know who not to invite. And there's Monroe's family and friends. Wonder if the church's going to hold everybody." She held up a sheet of paper so he could look at it. He saw that both sides were chock full of names.

"That sure is a lot of names," he said.

"I guess I'll invite some to the wedding and others to the reception."

"The backyard'll hold everybody," Robin told her.

"Yes," Aunt Belle said. "All the flowers out there near the house make everything look so pretty."

"I wanna know where the band's going to practice," Robin blurted out. "If we move to an apartment, there won't be room for all their drums and stuff."

39

"You have a good point there. Besides, in an apartment, the other tenants are bound to complain, call the music noise and such like that."

"I don't want him to sell the house."

"I don't, either. They don't make houses like this anymore. These days, they slap bricks and boards and paint together and call it a house. This house's been here a long time. And it can take it."

"Daddy told me to pack my things."

"Oh, dear, this is serious," Aunt Belle said thoughtfully. "Did you tell your father how you feel?"

"No. I didn't get a chance. He just kept telling me to be good and mind you."

"When he comes back, tell him. First thing. I'm sure things'll work out all right." She put her papers on the coffee table and hugged him.

That night before bed, Robin came down to say good night. Aunt Belle was working on her lists again. Watusi stood and stretched, then lay back on the sofa. Robin said, "I guess you and Monroe'll get your own house, too."

Aunt Belle did not look up. She scribbled into one of her notebooks. "Yes. Yes, somewhere in Wheeling. We'll probably move there right after we get back from Jamaica."

"Are you still going to keep me after you get married? When my father is away, I mean?"

She did not answer right away. Robin waited. He stood straight, then put his hands into his robe pockets.

She looked at him. Her right hand was raised, the fountain pen poised over the page she'd been writing on. She said, "Of course I will. Why do you ask? I'm getting married, not moving to the moon."

"I just wondered," Robin said. He poked at Watusi. The cat yawned and got up.

Robin was crossing the hallway to his bedroom when he heard Pollymae clawing at her cage.

Mindful of the weak floorboard on the landing, he went to the top of the stairs and listened. Pollymae was making an awful racket in her cage.

Aunt Belle said, "Robin . . . "

He started downstairs. He hadn't gotten to the bottom of the stairs before he heard a swooshing sound and saw Pollymae's shadow on the living room floor. She *had* been trying to get out, he thought. And somehow she had escaped from her cage.

Downstairs Robin went into the kitchen and got a butter knife. He banged it on top of Pollymae's cage. But Pollymae wouldn't fly back in. She soared around and around in the living room, enjoying her freedom. Robin knew he couldn't let her fly through the house all night, so he tried harder to coax her back into the cage.

Banging on the cage brought Watusi downstairs. He came into the living room to see what was going on. He sat in a corner, his head raised, watching Pollymae flying around the living room. Pollymae flew high and low. One time she even flew an inch or two from Watusi, but this startled Watusi so much, he skedaddled behind the sofa.

At one point, Pollymae soared around the ceiling light. Around and around she went. Robin got dizzy watching her. "I'll never get her back into the cage," he said. "Help me, Aunt Belle."

But even together, they couldn't catch Pollymae.

Robin got tired and stopped chasing Pollymae. He went to the sofa and flopped down. He stared after the parakeet, wondering what he should do. Pollymae's shadow on the wall looked like an airplane. All that was missing was the roar of an engine.

"Put some salt on her tail," Aunt Belle suggested.

Robin stared at his aunt. "I'm just going to have to wait until she gets tired of flying."

Pollymae was getting tired. She flew to the

top of the built-in bookcases and perched there and stayed. Robin thought she'd gone to sleep. He tiptoed to the bookcases, climbed up, and tried to grab Pollymae. Pollymae flitted away.

The parakeet circled the room again. Robin ran around chasing her.

In hiding, Watusi had turned brave. He eased his way from behind the sofa and lay on his stomach so he could watch Pollymae. Pollymae flew back to the top of the bookcases.

Robin eased over to the bookcases again. This time, he managed to touch Pollymae, but she flew out of his reach. She circled the living room again.

Pollymae wasn't flying as high as before. Maybe, Robin thought, she was looking for her cage. She was flying low enough so he wouldn't have to climb on furniture to catch her. He wished she wouldn't fly so fast.

Since Pollymae was flying lower, Watusi jumped up and followed her around the room.

"Catch her, boy!" Robin shouted to Watusi. "Maybe you'll have better luck than I did."

"Robin!" Aunt Belle said.

"Don't worry. He won't catch her. Nothing can catch that bird."

He went out onto the sun porch and took the bird cage off the hook. He brought it into the living room and set it on the floor. He sprinkled a handful of birdseed in front of the cage. That didn't work, either. Pollymae soared around the room. Robin dashed about, arms out, trying to make a lucky catch.

From the kitchen doorway, Aunt Belle said, "I wish that man had brought you goldfish. I bet you can swim better than you can fly." She started to laugh.

Robin didn't laugh. He looked at his aunt. Most of the time, he thought, she was a very nice old lady. He cleaned up the birdseed and put the cage back on its hook on the sun porch.

Standing in front of the cage on the sun porch, his hand still full of birdseed, the answer came to Robin. He smoothed the birdseed over his palm and started whistling. Softly at first, then louder. Pollymae flew over to him. She lit on his head, then flew down to the heel of his hand. She pecked at the birdseed. With his free hand, Robin gently grasped Pollymae. He put her into the cage. He dumped the seed from his hand into the little dish inside the bird cage. He fastened the cage door and dusted his hands. So that Pollymae didn't open the cage again, he tied it with an unbent paper clip Aunt Belle had given him. He swept the floor and scooped up birdseed and put it back into the box.

Robin wiped his brow with his arm and said, "Good night, Aunt Belle." He went upstairs to bed.

In his room, Robin turned down his bed, folding the bedspread neatly across the foot of the bed. Before he climbed in, he searched amid the things on his bureau for his night-light. He found it, crossed the room, plugged it in, and flicked off the overhead light.

The night-light in the baseboard outlet glowed and pushed back the darkness like a full moon.

He sat on the side of the bed. He was tired. He hadn't been that tired, hadn't used that much energy since he and the gang played a kickball game all the way through.

Kicking off his slippers, he lifted the sheet and climbed into bed.

Eight

ON Sunday, Robin and Aunt Belle went to eleven o'clock services at St. James AME church, the very church where his aunt was going to be married in a few weeks.

The weather had cooled off some and the wind was blowing. High in the top of trees, sparrows in fine voice sang loudly, reminding Robin of Pollymae. All she'd done since he'd coaxed her back into her cage was sing sing sing.

He and his aunt walked along, she clutching her wide-brim hat so it wouldn't blow off her head, Robin with his hands thrust deep into the pockets of his lightweight summer suit.

At the corner of their street, they turned and crossed over. The wind was blowing so hard, they had to walk backwards occasionally because of Aunt Belle's hat.

"This wind makes it seem like March," Aunt Belle said, as she backed along, holding onto her hat with both hands.

At last, when they got halfway to church, Aunt Belle snatched her hat off and carried it the rest of the way.

When they got to the church, she stood outside the basement entrance and put her hat on again. She ushered Robin in through the basement.

"Hey!" Robin shouted. "Where are we going? What's wrong with the front door?"

"Nothing," Aunt Belle said simply.

In the basement changing area, Robin broke away from his aunt and promptly got lost. He knew what she wanted, why they'd entered through the basement. He wasn't in any mood to sing in the choir. Never mind that he hadn't been to choir practice in a lot of weeks. He just wasn't ready to sing again. Yet.

Not only did Aunt Belle want him to sing, but Mr. Collins, the choir director, did, too.

Mr. Collins was a small man, only a few inches taller than Robin. "Oh, Sister Lazarus, how good of you to come. I know you brought your nephew."

47

Robin had hidden himself behind a group of teenage choir members. He heard his aunt say, " . . . around here somewhere."

They found him when the teenagers stepped into a secluded nook and started harmonizing, getting in a few bars of last-minute practice.

"Oh, there you are, Robin," Mr. Collins said. Robin had always thought that Mr. Collins looked like a walrus with his great handlebar mustache and the charcoal gray suit he always wore.

Robin hung his head and wished there was somewhere he could duck into. There was no place. He said, "Hi, Mr. Collins."

"Do you want to sing with us today?" Mr. Collins asked.

"Not really," Robin answered.

"Oh, I'll tell you what, Robin. Sing just this one Sunday. If you like it, come back to the choir. You're always welcome. You know that."

Robin didn't answer. He decided that if he'd known that it was Youth Choir Day, he would've pretended that he was sick, he wouldn't've come to church at all. But here he was. It was too late to do anything about that now. He went to Aunt Belle and stood in front of her. She shook out the choir robe she'd been holding and slipped it over Robin's head.

"Don't you look nice in your dark blue robe and your light blue slacks. And that red tie sticking out. You look like a little angel. Or a judge," she said.

Robin looked from Aunt Belle to Mr. Collins. He frowned at them both.

"One day you're going to thank me for this," Aunt Belle told him.

He pulled the robe down, adjusted it. He made one last effort to get out of singing. "Aunt Belle, how many times will I have to tell you I do not know how to sing?"

Robin went off into a corner without waiting for her to answer. He blinked back tears. The real reason was there; he tried not to think about it, but it surfaced in his mind.

It'd been the last day of school before Christmas vacation started. He'd hoped beyond hope that his mother would make it to his school to the recital his class gave. If she made it, he'd thought, then everything would be all right.

But she hadn't come. When he got home that day, he'd found out she'd gone into the hospital again. It hadn't been his fault, but he felt a lot of guilt because he'd been selfish wanting her with him. Just to hear him sing.

Aunt Belle came over to him, stood in front of him, her large body blocking out the light. He remembered where he was, why he was there. Aunt Belle said, "Your father is the greatest pianist in the world. Your mother had the

49

sweetest mezzo-soprano voice I've ever heard, and I've heard a lot. You come from a long line of choir singers. If your father hadn't gone to church, hadn't joined the choir, he never would've met your mother. We wouldn't be standing here having this conversation.

"You have a wonderful voice. Maybe you'll lose it when you get older, but you can sing. I've heard you when you thought no one was listening."

"How come you know I come from a long line? You must go back pretty far," he said, not caring whether he hurt her or not.

Her arms akimbo, Aunt Belle said, "Far enough."

He didn't get a chance to say anything else. It was time for the choir to line up. They lined up single-file — according to their heights — shortest ones leading. This made Robin the second one. The strains of "The Old Rugged Cross" began, and they marched upstairs.

Aunt Belle waited and followed the choir members upstairs. Then she took a seat in a front pew, where she wouldn't miss the hymns, wouldn't miss hearing Robin's voice.

Up in the choir section, Robin did not open his mouth. He stood there like a full-length picture on a wall; like a boy suddenly turned to stone. All around him he heard choir members singing. Some of them at the top of their lungs, some of them even off-key.

Without turning his head, he gave a sidelong glance around. But he couldn't figure out who was singing off-key. He did know he wasn't guilty. He hadn't opened his mouth.

Maybe the music moved him. Maybe he was embarrassed not to be singing while everybody else was, he didn't know. But the organist started another song and Robin didn't stand there like a bump on a log any longer. He opened his mouth. He sang.

Nine

AFTER services ended, and they were on the sidewalk, headed home, Aunt Belle said, "Didn't you enjoy that? See what you can do when you want to? When you really want to? Everybody enjoyed that. I watched them. When the choir sang that last song, there wasn't a dry eye in the house. And I heard your voice. You've got something powerful there."

Silently, Robin walked along beside her. She'd asked him a thousand questions. He didn't know which to answer first. If he said nothing, she'd think he was still mad at her, but he didn't care. It was her fault anyway. He didn't even want to go to church. He was already going to church on the last Saturday in August, not even three weeks away.

They walked along. The wind was still blowing, but not as hard as before. Aunt Belle didn't even have to remove her hat.

"Now you've got good news to tell your father tonight. When you talk to him about the house."

A gust of wind came up and blew Aunt Belle's hat off. Robin was going to chase it, but she motioned him back. "The way the wind's blowing, it's bound to blow it back," she told him. And it did. Robin caught it and handed it to her. They laughed at that, and Robin forgot all his troubles for the moment.

By the time he got home, he was sad again. Now they'd want him to sing in the choir all the time. Every Sunday. And every Thursday night they'd want him to go to choir practice.

In the living room, Aunt Belle pulled off her hat and flipped it onto the sofa, where Watusi was sleeping. Watusi woke up and thought the hat was a great new cat toy. He pounced on it at once. Aunt Belle seemed not to have noticed.

Robin slumped into the big chair by the window and watched Watusi play with his aunt's hat. Aunt Belle sat on the sofa and kicked off her shoes. "Either these feet are getting older or that church's moving farther away each Sunday." She leaned back and closed her eyes.

"Are you baking a cake for dessert?" Robin asked.

"Your father asked me that just before he left. I don't know yet."

Robin got Watusi off the sofa and took the hat away from him. Watusi, of course, didn't want to let it go.

"You need to go outside some," Robin said to Watusi, as he pried the cat's claws off the brim of the hat. "Stop, you bad thing." He carried Watusi through the house and opened the back door. Then he unhooked the screen door and put Watusi out into the backyard.

In the bird cage on the sun porch, Pollymae was sleeping on her perch. Robin glanced at her and went back into the living room.

Robin told Aunt Belle, "I'll be down to help you with the cake as soon as I change clothes."

He ran upstairs, skipping over steps so he could get to his room faster.

Ten minutes later, when he got downstairs again, Aunt Belle, too, had changed clothes and was tying one of his mother's aprons around her waist. The drawer next to the sink was full of aprons and things his mother had left there. His father hadn't gotten rid of them, although Mr. Lazarus never used an apron when he cooked.

"I don't know what time your father'll get

back, but I think I'd better make a big meal. I can always freeze the leftovers."

"Okay, what can I help you with first?" Robin asked. He didn't wait for his aunt to answer; instead, he went to the pantry and started taking things out for the cake. He had set out on the table everything he knew that went into a cake. "I hope there's milk." He went to the refrigerator. Just as he opened the door, it cranked up, clicked on, and reeled and rocked and whirred and roared and screeched. The whole kitchen vibrated.

When the noise subsided some, Aunt Belle said, "Are you hungry? Do you want something to eat?"

"No thanks. I'll just wait for cake."

"It's going to take a while. I'm going to make a pot roast with lots of carrots and celery and onions and little potatoes. Maybe a big salad. And some asparagus, I think," she said.

In the background, the refrigerator was still making a dreadful racket. The noise almost drowned out their voices. When the refrigerator clicked off and the kitchen was quiet again, Pollymae, awakened by the noise, started to sing.

"That fridge must be older than I am. I ought to have Monroe take a look at it one of these days."

"Daddy says it just needs defrosting when it does that. If that isn't what's wrong with it, can Monroe really fix it?"

"I hope. It certainly won't hurt to have him take a look at it." She went to the sink and filled a pan with water for the pot roast.

"Want me to unplug the fridge?" Robin asked.

"Go on. We might as well do everything. I wouldn't be able to sleep with that racket in here tonight. It woke me up twice last night."

No wonder she slept through the noise when I stepped on the weak floorboard, Robin thought. "I hope somebody can fix it," Robin said, as he unplugged the refrigerator.

The refrigerator hummed and whirred as it went off.

"Ah, peace and quiet," Aunt Belle said. "Last night, I thought I was in some kind of machine shop. I hope defrosting it helps." She set the pot with the roast in it on a back burner and turned it low. She started the cake. "Peel some potatoes, Robin. Make yourself busy."

"Oh, I forgot," he said. "I'd better get every-thing out of the fridge." He emptied the refrig-erator. By the time he had finished, the table was pretty well cluttered. "Looks like we'll have to eat in the dining room tonight."

"I'd say." Aunt Belle was mixing the ingre-dients for the cake by hand. When she got them blended together, she set the bowl under the electric mixer and switched it on.

"Chocolate is my favorite," Robin said.

"Your father's, too."

"Maybe you'd better make two cakes."

Aunt Belle made a face at him.

"I was just playing. Don't look at me like that."

"Speaking of playing, that reminds me of singing. When's choir practice?"

"Thursday night," Robin said. He rested his head on his hands, leaning on the table, watching what his aunt was doing. "How come playing makes you think of singing?"

"Well . . . "

She went to the pantry and got a bottle of vanilla, held it up to Robin. "I almost forgot the most important ingredient." She uncapped the bottle, measured a teaspoon of flavoring, and poured it into the batter. "I ought to make some corn pone. But I don't know what time your father'll get here."

His mouth watered as he thought of the little sticks of bread shaped like ears of corn.

Aunt Belle continued. "Speaking of music — "

"I thought we were talking about corn pone," Robin interrupted. The cluttered tabletop looked like the checkout counter at the supermarket, all covered with groceries. He pulled the bin of potatoes closer and went and got the peeler out of the cutlery drawer. He knelt on a chair and peeled potatoes. The chair was foamy soft. Soon after his mother had bought the dinette set, she'd started getting sick. He shook his head and tried to clear it. He concentrated on helping Aunt Belle fix Sunday dinner.

"Okay. The subject is music," Aunt Belle said in her finest schoolteacher voice. "With your interest in music, it should make you closer to your father. He's always liked music."

"You're a lot older than he is." Robin tried again to change the subject.

"Yes. Twelve years. What I'm trying to say is maybe he'll even come down to church and accompany you on a solo."

"Solo?"

"Yes. You know one of those songs where you get up and sing all by yourself."

"I know what one is. I just don't see me standing up there all by myself. Even if my father is playing the piano close by."

"There's nothing to be afraid of with that beautiful voice of yours. You share a voice like that. That's why God gave it to you. You didn't ask for it, did you?"

"No. And I don't want to sing solo. I don't want to sing with anybody, either," he said, as he peeled the last of the potatoes.

"I'm going to take three large ones for the pot roast. Can you cut them up for me? In tiny little chunks. Wash them and put them into a pot of water on the stove. Throw some eggs into the water with them."

While he was dropping eggs into the water, he told her, "Pretty soon, I'll be cooking as good as you." The cake, already in the oven, perfumed the kitchen. "That sure smells good."

"Don't it though?"

"Are you making chocolate icing?"

"I hadn't planned to, but get out the cocoa. You're driving me crazy with all this chocolate."

While she whipped the icing, Robin could barely keep his fingers out of the bowl. She'd slapped his hands a number of times before the icing was finished.

"Maybe I will make that corn pone."

Aunt Belle got a willow-blue mixing bowl out of the cupboard and mixed up the corn pone. Robin sat quietly at the table and smelled the cake and thought of how good it'd taste.

"You're kind of quiet," Aunt Belle said. "I like an assistant who'll chat with me."

"I was just thinking," he said. "Do you think my father misses my mother? A lot?"

Aunt Belle stopped stirring the corn pone batter. In mid-stir. She stared at Robin. He was seated on the opposite side of the table, his head resting on his hands. His big dark eyes stared into hers.

"Probably all the time," she said. "What makes you ask?"

"I don't know. I guess 'cause he hardly ever goes anywhere. Except to go play the piano. And one Saturday he left me out in the backyard playing kickball with my friends. He was gone a long time. We played four games and rested and he still hadn't come back."

"Maybe he went out . . . "

"I guess so," Robin said. "Later on when he took me to dinner, I saw broken flowers in the car. They were broken off, like the ones flower girls throw at weddings."

"Oh," Aunt Belle said. She studied Robin for a long, long time. "I hope he's planning on taking you to get a haircut for my wedding."

Robin saw that she'd changed the subject this time. "He said he would. Next week."

"See if some of the ice is loose in the freezer."

Robin leapt out of his chair and went to the fridge. A few pieces of ice had fallen. He took it out and put it into the sink.

"This is gonna take all night," he said. He remembered helping his mother defrost the refrigerator. She'd wanted to get a more modern one, one that never got frost in it. He stared at the mountains of frost in the freezer, then went back to the table and sat down.

Ten

THE roast was done and the cake was baked and frosted and it was almost time for Mr. Lazarus to come home. Aunt Belle had let Robin frost the cake. It had been the only way she could find to get his fingers out of the frosting bowl. The cake had gobs of frosting in some places and very little in others, but Robin thought it still looked good.

Everything was ready. Robin and Aunt Belle were taking little chunks of loose ice from the freezer and putting them into the sink.

Aunt Belle was saying, "We'll be in Jamaica soon now." She smiled. He thought she was overdoing it with the smiles. They almost blinded him. Her radiance was just that apparent.

Robin went back to the fridge and held out a bowl. Aunt Belle put more ice into it. "That sounds like Daddy," he said.

Outside, Raimi tooted the horn the way he always did, making a song out of it. Tires squealed as the van drew into the driveway.

Robin raced through the house and outside. He moved almost as fast as Pollymae had when she'd escaped from her cage the night before.

He stood on the porch and watched as the band members got out of the van. His father was first. Robin hopped off the porch, sped across the driveway, and hugged his father.

Mr. Lazarus lifted him up. "Good grief! You're getting big. Pretty soon, you'll be able to lift me up when I come home."

Robin smiled.

When his father put him down again, Robin said to the others, "Hi, Tex. Hi, Luther, Raimi."

They shook hands all around as if they hadn't seen one another the afternoon before. They went into the house.

"Something smells good in here," Raimi said.

Aunt Belle had come into the living room. "There's plenty. I hope everybody can stay. We won't get together like this often with me and Monroe in Wheeling."

"We weren't inviting ourselves to dinner," Luther said, fiddling with the saxophone strap.

"Speak for yourself," Raimi said, nudging Luther.

Aunt Belle laughed and said, "I know."

So they sat down to dinner. In the dining room. The kitchen table still looked like the checkout counter at the supermarket — loaded with groceries.

As for Robin, he'd felt happy to see his father again. But things were different now, somehow. No telling what'd happen, he thought, as he played with his salad and pot roast. Although he had wanted it, he only nibbled at the corn pone.

Although they hadn't really changed, even the band members seemed . . . different to Robin. He had a feeling that if he blinked the band members would disappear. He watched as they ate everything, even polishing off the boiled carrots and asparagus spears. He was grateful for that. He wouldn't have to worry about Aunt Belle serving them later in the week.

Maybe Aunt Belle had been right. They did seem like a part of the family. If the band broke up, he didn't know what he'd do. But they might. Tex had already said he wanted to go back to school, get a degree. Maybe even become an archaeologist. He glanced at Aunt Belle. She was looking at him. He knew that look. It meant that if he didn't make an attempt to eat some of his meal, he wouldn't get any cake. Not a crumb.

He perked up some and ate his food.

Aunt Belle brought in the cake. "Look what Robin and I baked," she said.

Sitting next to Robin, Luther stopped fiddling with the saxophone strap and tapped Robin on the shoulder. "This looks great. Just the thing to top off this meal."

"Thanks," Robin said.

Mr. Lazarus cut the cake and served it all around.

After they'd eaten the cake, Raimi tied on an apron. Robin recognized it as another one of his mother's.

"I'll wash," Luther said, and tucked the saxophone strap inside his shirt.

"No you won't," Raimi told him. "I like to wash dishes."

"One weird group," Robin muttered softly to himself.

He decided that things were even weirder when, shortly after the rest of them had gone into the living room, Raimi poked his head in and asked, "Should we finish defrosting this refrigerator, too?"

"I'll get that later," Aunt Belle said.

Raimi came into the living room. He wiped his hands on the apron.

"It's no problem," Raimi said. "The ice's already all melted."

"Let him do it," Mr. Lazarus said. "He thrives on work."

Raimi went back into the kitchen.

After Raimi and Tex and Luther finished in the kitchen, they joined the others in the living room. Robin went out to the kitchen. The first thing that he saw was the cake keeper on the table. He lifted the lid. There was one small sliver of cake in the midst of a pile of chocolate crumbs.

He grabbed the last slice of cake and ate it. He looked around the kitchen again. Everything was spotless. They'd even put the groceries back into the fridge. Someone with a white glove couldn't've found a cleaner kitchen. The refrigerator gleamed like new. The only sign of its great age was the sound it made as it cranked up and clicked on. It was quieter now, but defrosting hadn't helped much.

He crossed to the sink, washed and dried the cake keeper, and set it on its shelf in the pantry. Raimi had left the apron hanging on the back of a chair. Robin folded it and returned it to the drawer. He looked around the kitchen again and shook his head. "Grown-ups are weird," he said, and went back into the living room.

His father was sitting on the corner of the

sofa. Robin went over to him and sat astraddle the arm of the sofa.

"That was some meal," Raimi was saying to Aunt Belle.

Tex said, "You outdid yourself this time."

"I had help. I couldn't've done it without Robin."

"Well," Luther said. He twiddled the saxophone strap. "Charles, where are we off to next? I mean after the wedding."

"Oh, I don't know." Charles Lazarus leaned forward and laced his fingers together across his knees. "I don't want to do anything to conflict with Belle's wedding. Maybe I ought to hang it up. I can find something else to do as a sideline to teaching."

Robin had heard his father talk about giving up his weekend jobs before. But it had never happened. So far.

"Let's concentrate on the wedding," Mr. Lazarus went on. "We have to supply something special. We've got to practice like crazy. Every spare moment, I think."

"Yeah, yeah," Raimi agreed. He was sitting on one side of the big hassock. Tex sat on the other side.

Fiddling with his saxophone strap, Luther said, "Upbeat stuff."

Tex got off the hassock and came around and stood in front of the group. He said, "I've been

working on something that might be appropri-
ate. It's still a little rough — "

"Let's hear it," Mr. Lazarus said excitedly.

"I'd rather not. Not right now." Tex got his
cowboy hat off the end table. "Let's see —
we'll practice Wednesday night. I'll have it ready
then. I've got to go." He moved toward the
door. "See you."

Robin walked Tex out onto the porch. "Are
you really going back to school?" Robin asked.

"I'm afraid so. I've put it off for a long time.
I might as well start finishing some of the things
I start. Like that song. I've been working on it
off and on. Picked it up last week. I still like it.
I'd like to finish it as part of my wedding present
to the happy couple."

Robin frowned. Somebody was always men-
tioning the wedding. More and more, it looked
like it was going to happen. And tomorrow —
not three weeks from now, he thought.

Tex was saying, "Maybe I'll go to school right
here in town. I don't want to give up playing
my guitar in the band. Unless we break up."

Robin and Tex shook hands. Before he put
on the cowboy hat, Tex fanned Robin with it.

Robin stayed on the porch until Tex had
disappeared down the block and headed into
the settlement.

Tex's words had left Robin just as concerned
about the band. All he knew was that Tex did

not want to give up playing his guitar in the band.

Robin slumped down on the top step. He noticed that already it had started getting dark earlier. But it wasn't too dark to see that he and his father would have to cut the grass before the wedding.

He went back into the house. Luther and Raimi were getting ready to leave.

"Take care, Robin," Luther said.

"That was delicious cake," Raimi said as he and Luther went out.

"Good night," Robin told them. The screen door slapped shut behind them. Robin fastened its hook.

"It's been quite an evening," Aunt Belle said. She rose and moved toward the stairs. "Good night, all." She started upstairs, stopped, and turned. To Robin she said, "Don't stay up too late." She went upstairs.

"I won't," he said, and sat astraddle the arm of the sofa. He looked over his father's shoulder and saw that he was scribbling notes in a music manuscript book. "Are you really going to sell the house?"

Mr. Lazarus scratched out a whole bar of notes that he didn't like and wrote in others. Then he put his pen aside and looked at his son. Robin gripped the arm of the sofa with both hands as if to draw strength from it.

"I know you don't want to move," his father said. "Why not?"

Robin didn't answer. He couldn't. How could he really explain the way he felt? He didn't think he really wanted to explain. He thought it'd sound crazy, but he knew he had to tell his father something. He searched for words.

"I just don't . . . want to," Robin said. He realized this was as bad as not having made a comment at all. He took a deep breath, then closed his eyes. He opened his eyes again and looked at his father. Mr. Lazarus sat with his long slender fingers laced together around his knees. Robin opened his mouth to say exactly what he felt, but his father started scribbling notes again, humming the tune to himself as he wrote.

Mr. Lazarus stopped humming. He murmured, "Better make this B natural."

Robin got up and started upstairs. When he'd climbed three steps, he looked back at his father. Mr. Lazarus had not even noticed that Robin was no longer sitting on the arm of the sofa.

Eleven

R$_{\text{IGHT}}$ before he woke up, Robin dreamed about his mother. She appeared in the dream, her usual cheerful self. All she'd said to him was, "Be natural." This had alarmed Robin. He'd lain in bed clutching the covers until he'd gone back to sleep.

When he awakened again, he'd forgotten the dream. He got up and went downstairs. He could already hear Aunt Belle stirring about in the kitchen.

He heard her humming to herself as she fried bacon and brewed coffee. He could hear the wire whisk strike against the sides of the mixing bowl as she beat eggs to scramble.

"Good morning," Robin said cheerfully as he

went through the kitchen and out to the sun porch to feed and water Pollymae and Watusi.

"You sound awfully happy this morning," his aunt said.

He didn't answer. He opened the screen door and looked out. A big orange sun blasted down heat rays. Another August dog day.

The sun, warm on his face like that, reminded him of his mother. She used to make a fire in the fireplace in the winter. And the sun's rays were like one of her fires. He remembered one time she couldn't find a match and the pilot light on the stove had gone out. She'd made a fire by rubbing two sticks together. Just like she'd learned when she was a Girl Scout, when she was twelve years old. He'd tried to make a fire in the fireplace like that, but he never could.

From the kitchen, Aunt Belle said, "I've called you twice. Your eggs are getting cold. Your orange juice is getting warm. Your milk's curdling."

He went to the table and sat down and sampled his food. It was good.

"Did you talk to your father?" Aunt Belle asked as she sat opposite him. She poured herself a cup of coffee and put jam on a piece of toast.

"Kind of," he said.

She sipped her coffee and said, "Robin, what does 'kind of' mean?"

71

"I was going to, but Daddy kept on writing some kind of music. So I just went to bed and left him there."

"No wonder he's sleeping in," Aunt Belle said. "And I got up before you."

"Huh?" Robin stopped eating, a puzzled look on his face.

"I want to get an early start. You know Monroe and I are going over to Wheeling for a couple of days."

"How long will you be gone, exactly?"

"Don't look like that. I've seen a happier face on someone who fell down and skinned his knee. We'll be back before you know we're gone."

Something she said made him remember his dream. "I dreamed about my mother last night," he said. "All she said in my dream was, 'Be natural.' But I woke up scared from it."

Thoughtfully Aunt Belle said, "Must be some kind of message."

"That's what Daddy said before I went to bed last night," Robin told her. "He kept muttering, 'B natural.'"

"Then it's got something to do with music." Aunt Belle sipped coffee again. "She's got to be trying to send a message. Maybe she's saying 'act naturally.' You did mention you didn't say exactly what you wanted to your father. Just be Robin. Charles is kind of stubborn. But he's

72

listening when he acts like he isn't. I know my brother. You should just walk up to your father and talk to him just like you're talking to me."

"I wish he'd come down to breakfast," Robin said.

As if he'd heard them talking about him, Charles Lazarus came downstairs, but not before he'd stepped smack-dab in the middle of the weak floorboard.

In the house, in the early morning silence, the floorboard sounded like a dynamite blast. Robin put down his fork and clamped his hands over his ears in mock pain. "Ouch!" he said.

Looking sleepy and as if he hadn't heard a thing, Mr. Lazarus came into the kitchen, seated himself at the table, and poured a cup of coffee. He reached for the newspaper. Robin realized it was now or never, before his father buried himself in the morning paper.

"Did you sleep okay?" Robin asked.

"Yes. Great. I guess I'm still a little tired, though."

Robin pushed his empty plate aside and rested his head on his hands on the table.

Robin said, "I don't want to move. Leave my friends. And I don't know how the whole band's gonna practice in an apartment. . . ."

His father was more awake now. He said, "I really am thinking about giving it up. I'm too old to keep knocking around the way I am."

73

Grown-ups, Robin thought, talked too much about getting old. He remembered how touchy Aunt Belle was about her age.

"You love music too much," he said simply.

"Yes. But sometimes we have to let go of what we love."

Robin got the feeling that his father wasn't talking about music at all.

"I might have to give up Watusi." As an afterthought he said, "And Pollymae. And I don't wanna."

Aunt Belle said, "I've told you that all along, Charles. I don't mean to meddle, but I care about Robin. Like a son."

Mr. Lazarus blinked and looked at her. He said, "I thought you and Monroe were going off to Wheeling, shopping or something."

"Are you trying to get rid of me?" Aunt Belle teased.

Mr. Lazarus laughed and said, "Not my favorite sister."

"I'm also your only sister."

"Even if I had a whole slew of sisters, you'd still be my favorite."

Embarrassed, Aunt Belle smiled and said, "Thanks."

Outside a car horn tooted. Aunt Belle got up. "That's Monroe." She pinched Robin's cheek and added, "You need a haircut. You won't come to my wedding like that, will you? Your hair's longer than mine." She went into the living room and got her suitcase out of the corner by the door. "See you soon," she said, and opened the screen door.

Monroe had come up onto the porch. He took the bag from Aunt Belle. "How's everybody?" he said.

"Okay," Robin mumbled.

"How you doing?" Mr. Lazarus asked.

After Aunt Belle and Monroe had gone out, Robin went into the living room and slumped into a corner of the sofa, nearest the door. As Monroe and Aunt Belle went down the steps, he heard Monroe say, "Let's stop and get our picture taken. You know, a sort of before-and-after shot." They laughed.

Robin raised himself up and looked out through the big picture window. He glanced out just in time to see his aunt give Monroe a playful shot in the arm. He looked out of the window until they had gotten into Monroe's car and roared away. Their laughter still rang in his ears.

Twelve

IT was seven days before the wedding. Aunt Belle and Monroe were still in Wheeling. They had offered to take Robin with them, but his father had said no.

"There's no getting around it," Mr. Lazarus said. "Someone else will have to stay with you once in a while. I have commitments to honor until Labor Day." He strode around the room as he talked. Robin was slumped on the sofa, Watusi sleeping at his side. Out on the sun porch, Pollymae sang her head off.

Mr. Lazarus went on. "Belle certainly can't stay with you while she's in the Bahamas."

"She's going to *Jamaica,*" Robin said. But his father, as usual, wasn't listening.

"I've got a lady named Isola Humpheries coming by. She comes highly recommended. She should be here soon."

Almost before his father had finished speaking, Isola Humpheries rapped at the screen door. "Hello?" she sang out.

"Come in," Mr. Lazarus said.

"No," Isola sang through the screen door. "I think it's latched."

"Robin, get that."

He pulled himself off the sofa, padded to the door, and unhooked it. Isola Humpheries was not only tall but wide, too. Robin gaped at her, then remembered it wasn't polite to stare.

"Hello," he said, as he held the door open.

"Are you the young fella I'll be sitting with?"

"Yes." She came into the living room and Robin latched the door.

The room seemed smaller with Isola there. Robin noticed that she'd had to bend down to come in, just as Monroe had. He saw that Isola had a voice that sang no matter what she said. Her skin was a light-brown color, her hair cut so close that her head looked as round as Benny's new kickball. A round, fuzzy kickball, Robin thought. He remembered what Aunt Belle had said about his hair being longer than hers. Looking up at Isola, he saw that his hair *was* lots longer than hers.

"Please sit down," Robin said. He watched

77

Isola lower her generous frame into the big chair by the bookcases. He and his father could sit in the chair together, side by side, with room to spare, but Isola hung over the sides of it.

"Isn't he precious?" Isola said. "Got the cutest little dimples and the prettiest big brown eyes I ever saw."

Robin hunched down in a corner of the sofa. Oh, brother, he thought. Why can't she just call me kid, like Monroe does?

Mr. Lazarus said, "I'll be out most of the night." He went to the telephone table and scribbled on the pad that was there. "Here's the number where I can be reached in an emergency. I don't like to leave him alone at night."

"You mentioned you'd have to go out of town sometimes. . . ."

"Yes. I won't be going next weekend. My sister's getting married on Saturday and I'll be staying pretty close to home."

"I see," Isola said, her arms folded across her ample chest. She rocked gently back and forth. "I think I've got it all."

Mr. Lazarus went upstairs. When he came down again, he carried a portfolio of sheet music. "I'm not sure what time I'll be home," he said, and pinched Robin's cheek. He went out.

After Mr. Lazarus left, Isola turned on the TV. Robin was left to his own devices. For him, that didn't include watching reruns of action shows. Some of the shows hadn't been hits; he hadn't liked them when they were new and he didn't like them now. He and his mother had spent time watching reruns of situation comedies, her favorite.

Robin played with Watusi a bit, then changed the newspaper lining the bottom of Pollymae's cage. When he'd done this, he tried to teach Pollymae how to talk. It wasn't a simple job.

He draped a hood over the cage like Tex said, and put one end of the hood over his head. "Hello," he said, standing in front of the cage. He repeated that one word, *hello,* over and over again. His throat started to get dry. Pollymae responded with a throaty squawk. She started singing again. Robin gave up and left her alone.

He went outside and sat on the steps with Watusi. He didn't understand how Isola could stand being cooped up in the house on a hot evening like this. But there wasn't much air circulating outside, either. He thought about her but couldn't tell whether he liked her or not. But he did know she certainly was no Aunt Belle.

Isola came to the back door. "Are you hungry?" she asked.

"No. Not yet. I think I'll take a nap," he told her and got up.

He went upstairs and lay on his bed without turning down the covers. How his mother'd hated for him to do that. He crossed his feet at the ankles, and stared at the ceiling.

It was even hotter in the room. He wondered if he should've stayed outdoors. The window was open, but the thin little breeze didn't do anything more than rustle the curtains.

Although he couldn't be sure, he must've dozed off. When he awakened and looked at the window, it was very dark. He heard the TV downstairs and wondered if Isola'd moved from the spot where he'd left her. He got up and went downstairs.

Isola was still in the same place on the sofa, but she was also knitting. It was a long blue thing that looked like some kind of rug. She smiled at Robin as he went through the living room and out onto the sun porch.

Pollymae swung on her perch. She cocked her head to one side and eyed Robin. "You wanna get out?" he said, going to the cage. He unfastened the paper clip and opened the cage. Instantly, Pollymae flew out and into the living room. Robin went in and sat on the hassock. Pollymae swooped down, inches from Isola's head.

"Lord have mercy!" Isola exclaimed, dropping her knitting. Her hands spread like wings.

"I have to let her out every once in a while. I guess she feels too cooped up in that cage," Robin explained.

Pollymae flew around the room. Isola glanced sideways at the bird. Pollymae flew to the top of one of the bookcases. Isola got her knitting off the floor. "She almost scared me to death. And I heard you out there talking to her. My nerves must be getting bad."

"Her name is Pollymae. I named my cat Watusi after some African warriors I saw on TV one time."

Isola went back to her knitting. "How long are you going to let him — er, her — fly 'round like that?"

"Not long. I want her to stretch her wings."

Without losing a knit or a purl, Isola's knitting needles began to fly. The long blue thing grew longer.

After a few minutes of flying, Pollymae surprised Robin and flew back into her cage. When he went in to fasten the door, Pollymae was eating birdseed that'd spilled over onto the newspaper in the bottom of her cage.

"Good girl," Robin said, and fastened the cage door.

*   *   *

The next day, Sunday, it rained, a late summer drizzle that made the air steamy. Although Robin was pretty much housebound most of the day, around one-thirty the rain stopped. The sun blazed down like spun gold. As soon as he saw it he went to the telephone and called Benny.

"What you doing?" he asked as soon as Benny came on the line.

"Nothing. What you doing?"

"Nothing." He hesitated only a moment. He had spent enough time indoors and wanted to get out. It was like he was Pollymae, cooped up in a cage. He had to do something. Get his mind off things. "Let's play kickball."

Obviously, Benny wanted to get out, too, but he said, "The grass's too wet."

"It'll be dry by the time we get the gang all rounded up," Robin said.

So they got together for a game of kickball on the last Sunday afternoon before the wedding.

Although the sun was blazing, the grass was still a bit damp. "This is better than staying in all day," Robin said to Benny.

"Yeah," Benny agreed.

Cyndy was there, too. And the twins. Cyndy was being especially nice, not bossy at all.

"Are you in the wedding?" Cyndy asked Robin.

"No," Robin said. "And I don't wanna be."

He realized his words had been too sharp. He smiled to try to tone them down some.

Cyndy hadn't noticed, or hadn't cared. She said, "If it was my aunt, I would've been a flower girl."

Aunt Belle had wanted him to be an usher, or the ring bearer. Something. But it was too late for that now. She'd already gotten somebody else. "I didn't want to be in it," Robin said, softly. "I'm just glad Aunt Belle's getting married." He wondered if he should get a nice gift for them. After all, Monroe had brought him Pollymae. Maybe he *would* get them something — something very nice.

Somebody kicked the ball. Robin should've caught it, but he didn't. It shot through his outstretched arms like a rocket.

I'd better think about a gift later, Robin thought, before my team loses this game.

Then he realized the game hadn't really started. It was just a warm-up exercise.

Someone tossed the ball back to Benny. He dribbled it on the walkway. On the sun porch, Pollymae started singing. Watusi scratched at the screen door to be let out. Robin opened it for him.

Once outside, Watusi went to the hedges and stretched out on the damp grass in the shade.

"Let's play kickball," Terry and Barry, the twins, said together. One of them grabbed the ball from Benny in mid-dribble. He tossed it to the other twin.

Benny yelled, "Hey! Terry!"

"I'm Barry," the slender boy said, as he dribbled the ball.

"Whoever you are. Come on, let's just play kickball."

Before they started the game, Benny said, "Hey, Robin, let's split the twins up. One on each team. I want Barry." Benny pointed to a twin. "Okay, Barry. You're on my team now."

"I'm Terry. We can't split up. I have to play with Barry."

"No you don't. Just for one game," Benny pleaded.

Reluctantly, one twin played on each team. In the end, that hadn't been such a good idea. They both played badly because, as Robin soon saw, Barry didn't want to beat Terry and Terry didn't want to beat Barry. That game ended in a draw.

They rested on the steps before starting another game. But they never did play. Instead, soon, they started going home. Cyndy was the last to leave. She started through the break in the hedges, turned, and said, "No game Saturday. It's the wedding." She patted her hair and added, "I'm going to the beauty shop. My mother's getting my hair curled. 'Bye."

Robin sat on the steps, leaning against the

screen door, and watched them leave. Since there wasn't a kickball game next Saturday, he realized he probably wouldn't see any of them until the wedding. Or the reception.

Robin stood up. Watusi dashed over to the steps. Robin opened the screen door and Watusi ran inside. Slowly, Robin went inside, too. He wondered when his father was going to take him to get a haircut.

Thirteen

ON Monday night, Robin's father had a dinner date.

It was a clear night and the dog-day heat wave hadn't let up.

Aunt Belle and Monroe were busy with last-minute wedding business. Since Mr. Lazarus's date had also been last minute, Isola couldn't stay with Robin.

Mr. Lazarus came downstairs around seven o'clock, dressed to go out. "The sitter didn't get here yet, huh?" he asked Robin.

From where Robin was slumped on the sofa, he said, "Isola's coming?"

"No," his father said. "It's someone else."

He adjusted his tie and grinned at Robin, who was watching a rerun of a situation comedy.

"Who, then?" Robin asked.

Mr. Lazarus looked at his watch. "In a minute."

There was a rap at the screen door. From where he was on the sofa, Robin couldn't see who was at the door.

"It's open," Mr. Lazarus said.

Robin sat up. "This is the sitter?" he said, as Tex came inside carrying a brown portfolio and his guitar and amplifier.

Tex stood in the doorway and set the guitar and amp by the door. He took off his cowboy hat and fanned Robin with it. He tossed the hat on the corner of the lamp table.

"Well, what are we going to do tonight?" Tex asked Robin after Mr. Lazarus had left.

"I don't know," Robin said.

Since it was summer there were wall-to-wall reruns on TV. The last of the situation comedies had gone off. He really didn't have any idea what to do. If Aunt Belle had been staying with him, she would've had him cooking something or cleaning something. Or else she'd talk to him all night about her wedding. He smiled to himself, remembering.

"I know," Robin said. "Let's go down to the mall. I've wanted to go, but it's been too hot to do much of anything. I've been saving my allowance.''

Tex looked at his watch. "Okay. Stores are always open late in the mall. And it's air-conditioned. Let's go.'' Tex stood up and got his cowboy hat from the lamp table.

Robin rose and raced upstairs.

When he came down again, Tex was in the kitchen making sure the door was locked. He got the keys off the rack on the kitchen wall and went back into the living room.

"All set?''

"All set,'' Robin answered.

At the mall, Robin had selected a present he knew Aunt Belle would like. Maybe Monroe would, too. Before Tex and Robin headed home, they stopped in an ice cream parlor and had cones of strawberry ice cream, Robin's favorite.

"Will you be a teacher when you get out of school, Tex?''

"Oh, I don't know. I'd like to work outdoors sometimes.''

Robin knew what that meant. He'd collected rocks for a project at school once. Tex was going to have to travel all over the world digging up rocks. This must mean, Robin thought, that the band really is breaking up.

"... I don't know, though,'' Tex was saying.

"I'd like to do something that'll keep me close to home. Maybe I'll be an astronomer."

"You like science," Robin said, and Tex nodded. They ate in silence for a while. Then Robin said, "Everything's different now. Aunt Belle's getting married. I got a new sitter. You're the best sitter I've had since Aunt Belle, Tex." Some of his ice cream dripped down the side of the cone. Robin licked it off. "The band breaking up — "

"Hold it. Hold it. Who told you that, your father?" Tex held his hand up, the palm facing Robin.

Robin nodded.

Tex laughed and said, "Charles's been saying that ever since we played our first job. Even if I do go away to school, I'm not going that far away. I'll still play on weekends. We'd probably still get together for our weekly jam sessions." Tex shook his head. "Your father always says that. I think he thinks it makes us play better or something."

"Then I shouldn't worry about that?"

"I wouldn't if I were you," Tex said. They finished their ice cream and left the store.

Fourteen

TIME was running out, and Robin realized his father still hadn't taken him to get a haircut. But he needn't have worried. The job went to Aunt Belle. That Friday morning, the day before the wedding, Mr. Lazarus had dressed and had left the house at nine o'clock.

At ten o'clock, Aunt Belle said, "Come on, Robin. That man must have a thousand things on his mind. I'm the one who should be nervous and forgetful." She ushered Robin outside to her sky-blue Hyundai.

Once in the car, the first thing Aunt Belle did was to blast the air conditioner. Robin wished he'd thought to bring a jacket, or at least had worn a long-sleeved shirt. He looked at his aunt, cool and crisp, dressed in a white sleeveless outfit. He shivered. Gooseflesh had already started to rise on his arms, but Aunt Belle's arms were as smooth as brown silk.

The barbershop wasn't crowded. Aunt Belle waited on a plastic chair, skimming *Newsweek* and *Ebony* and *Jet* while Robin got his haircut.

Afterward they got back into the Hyundai and went out on the open road.

"Do you have some more wedding errands?" Robin asked.

"No. Everything's done. If it isn't, it's too bad now. Why?"

"This isn't the way to go home."

Aunt Belle looked at him, then concentrated on her driving.

They went along Forbes Avenue. Cemeteries stretched for several blocks on one side of Forbes. Robin did not want to look out the window, but he did.

Aunt Belle shifted gears and got into the right-hand lane, ready to make a turn.

But she did not make a turn. Instead, she parked on Forbes and they got out. Robin waited in a grassy area where a sidewalk should've been, while Aunt Belle reached into the car and got her suitcase-sized purse off the backseat.

She hefted the purse to her shoulder and locked the car. "Okay, let's go."

In silence, they walked into the cemetery, through the wrought-iron gate.

They made their way along a cobblestone path. They hadn't walked very far when Robin saw a man, his head bent, staring at one of the cemetery markers.

Although he was still a good way off, he saw that it was his father.

Robin raced to Mr. Lazarus's side. His father turned and looked at Robin. Robin looked back and saw that Aunt Belle had not followed him.

"Daddy . . ." he said.

Mr. Lazarus grasped Robin's hand. Only then did Robin look down at the grave. He had not seen it before. They had not let him go to the cemetery back then. Now he looked at the brass marker on his mother's grave and read the inscription:

TRACY UNDERWOOD LAZARUS

it said. And the day she was born and the day she died. Nothing more.

In his mind's eye he'd imagined she had a high headstone and a concrete slab covering her grave, just like in an old cowboy movie, or a horror film he'd seen.

It should've said more, Robin thought. He read it over and over again.

At last Mr. Lazarus said, "Are you ready?"

They walked out of the cemetery. Robin was still holding his father's hand; gripping it, really. He realized how tight he held his father's hand and relaxed it some.

Mr. Lazarus had walked over to the cemetery. He had planned to ride back on the bus, the 61 A East Pittsburgh, if he got too tired to walk back. But Aunt Belle practically ordered him to get behind the wheel of the sky-blue Hyundai.

Robin's father was tall and sat scrunched over the steering wheel. Robin stared at his father's hands, long piano player's fingers gripping the steering wheel.

When Mr. Lazarus had tooled the car back into traffic, he said, "I thought that you should see . . . your mother's grave."

"How come you didn't take me with you before?"

Mr. Lazarus's fingers opened and closed on the steering wheel. He twisted around and glanced at Robin, then back at the street. He said, "I don't know. I guess today I felt it was right. I called Belle and asked if she'd bring you along. . . . She reminded me that I hadn't taken you to get a haircut. That's a great haircut."

"Thanks," he said. Robin didn't know what else to say. He glanced out the window. They'd left the cemetery behind. He turned to his father again. "Thanks."

They rode in silence the rest of the way.

When they arrived home, Robin leapt out of the car as soon as his father had set the hand brake. He ran across the yard and up onto the porch. Then he suddenly realized he still had a lot to do before the wedding. He had to shine his shoes, get used to his new haircut. Most of all, he had to decide what to wear. The wedding was still twenty-four hours away, but Robin was getting excited now. He wanted everything to go right.

As he raced through the living room, headed for the stairs, he heard Pollymae let out a squawk that sounded an awful lot like, "Hello." He couldn't be sure. He stopped and listened, but she didn't utter another sound. He went upstairs.

It was too hot to stay in the house and polish his shoes. He brought them outdoors and sat on the front steps. He also wanted to look at the flowers. If he and his father moved, they would leave them there for the next family.

While he dabbed polish on his Sunday shoes, he glanced over at the old tire his mother had put out into the yard, with a flower planted inside of it. He'd helped her paint the top half of the tire white. The flower she'd planted in it was a verbena. She'd let him do most of the painting, and he'd gotten more paint on himself than he had on the tire. She'd helped him wash the paint off with turpentine. Sitting out on the steps like that, when a breeze came up, he could almost smell the odor of turpentine. If the breeze was strong enough, he could also smell the scent of verbena.

Fifteen

THE scent of freshly mowed grass wafted its way up to Robin's room on Saturday. He had slept with the window wide open because it had been another scorchingly hot night. It was finally the Saturday of the wedding.

Robin crossed to the window and looked out. There wasn't a cloud in the sky. It wouldn't rain on the day Aunt Belle got married after all, he thought.

He got dressed. He had to go to the pet shop to get a box of birdseed for Pollymae. Watusi had already finished eating and was lying on the foot of Robin's bed.

As he went past the foot of the bed, he patted Watusi's stomach. Watusi rolled over and over.

Out in the hallway, Robin walked carefully, avoiding the weak floorboard, and bounded down the steps two at a time.

He went out through the kitchen.

He was closer to the shopping center when he went through the back way. He went through the break in the hedges and up the walk.

Twenty minutes later, when he returned, he heard the band members downstairs tuning their instruments. He knew they liked to get in some last-minute practice when they had an extra-special engagement to play.

After Robin had fed and watered Pollymae, he sat on the back steps, Watusi at his side. Down in the cellar, the band revved up and started jamming.

In her cage, on the ledge in the sun porch, Pollymae started squawking. Robin twisted around and pressed his head against the screen door to peep in at her. Pollymae wouldn't stop fluttering, wouldn't stop squawking. Robin got up and went inside to check on her.

"What's the matter?" he asked, his face close to the bird cage.

Pollymae didn't stop squawking.

Robin could not find anything that was wrong. Maybe the music was getting to her; maybe it was too loud; maybe she was nervous. He hoped she wasn't sick. In the end he took the cage off the ledge and carried it upstairs to his room.

He closed the door. Closed them off from the sound of the music.

Of course, they could still hear the music, but not like before. Anyhow, Pollymae stopped squawking. In the room with the door closed and the window open and a breeze coming in, Robin felt like he was in a giant bird cage, sealed off, insulated a little.

He stayed in his room until the band had practiced as much as they could, as much as they wanted to — which was quite a lot and a long time.

When he'd gone to the mall on Monday with Tex, Robin had bought wrapping paper. He used it now to wrap the present he'd bought for Aunt Belle and Monroe.

After the present was wrapped, and the band had stopped practicing, and the other members had gone home to get ready for the wedding, Robin took Pollymae downstairs.

On the sun porch again, she started singing happily.

Even on her wedding day, Aunt Belle had mentioned fixing lunch for Robin and his father. Robin had said he wasn't hungry. "I just want wedding cake," he said, rubbing his stomach.

"You can really eat some cake, can't you?" Aunt Belle said.

"It's my favorite food." Robin glanced at the

big clock on the living-room mantelpiece. "Shouldn't you start getting ready?"

Aunt Belle gave a nervous little laugh. She said, "I've got plenty of time." But she did go upstairs and started getting ready.

Robin and his father got dressed, too. He certainly didn't want to be late for his own aunt's wedding.

By ten after four, everybody was ready. Hands in his pockets, Robin admired once again the spit shine he'd put on his Sunday oxfords.

Raimi drove them in Mr. Lazarus's car. Robin sat up front, and Mr. Lazarus and Aunt Belle sat in the back. Raimi threw the car into gear and roared up the street and around the corner to St. James AME Church.

Sixteen

ROBIN sat in the front pew between his great-aunt Dorinda from Detroit, Michigan, and her daughter, Esther. They had said he should sit with them for company. He hadn't yet started to fidget. If it was hot in the church, he knew he'd get restless. He twisted around and stole a glance at the back. There wasn't an empty space to be seen. He was looking for Benny. He found him sitting in the center pew. Benny nodded to Robin. Robin nodded back and continued scanning the crowd. It looked as if everybody in town had been invited. He faced front again and waited for the ceremony to start.

Outside, a summer wind rattled the stained-glass windowpanes. But Robin could tell by the way the sun streamed in through the figures on the windows that it wasn't going to turn cloudy. Aunt Belle had said she'd call the whole thing off if it rained. If it even drizzled.

At the first strains of the somber wedding music, Robin looked down the aisle. He wished they'd play wedding music on the piano. The organ made it sound sad to Robin. It sounded like a funeral. He clasped his hands together and waited.

Suddenly, Mr. Lazarus dashed through the side door and approached Robin. "The ring bearer got sick," his father said. "Come on." His father started back through the church. Robin followed him.

In the room off the choir area, Mr. Lazarus said, "Can you do it? Do you know what to do? I wish we'd rehearsed more. I wish I'd made you do it from the first. Your mother would've. You're Belle's favorite nephew. You ought to be in the wedding anyhow. I don't know what we were thinking." His father's words came out in a rush.

Robin faced his father. He thought that his father sounded like a madman. Robin stood with his hands in his pockets. In my sleep, Robin thought. I could do it in my sleep. He'd paid close attention at the rehearsal. "Daddy," Robin said, "I can do it."

Robin took his hands out of his pockets, and Mr. Lazarus thrust the little cushion with the rings on top of it into Robin's hands. He tweaked Robin's nose.

Taking long strides, Mr. Lazarus led Robin out through a side door.

Outside, the wind had picked up. There still wasn't any sign of rain. The sun continued to sparkle down like it was being reflected off millions of gold coins. A hot, mighty wind rustled the leaves. It was like any other August dog-day Saturday, except for the wind.

At the front of the church, Robin noticed the wind was stinging Aunt Belle's eyes. He saw her reach under the veil and wipe tears away.

Over the wind, they heard the music. Mr. Lazarus and Aunt Belle linked arms and marched into the church.

Inside, from doorway to altar, Robin thought the distance had somehow grown. Or maybe it was because he had to walk so slowly.

They got to the altar.

At the altar, he took the rings out of his pocket and set them back on top of the cushion. He'd moved them because he was afraid he'd drop them in the grass or something.

But nothing bad had happened, at least not so far.

Reverend Maryland said, "Dearly Beloved, we are gathered here in the sight of God to

unite this man and this woman in holy matri-
mony."

Robin only half listened to the reverend's
singsong voice. It reminded him of Isola. Without
turning his head, Robin tried to look out over
the pews. He was sure he'd heard Cyndy giggle.
There were so many faces, he couldn't find any
of his friends.

The minister went on: "If there's anyone here
who thinks this man and this woman should not
be joined, let him speak now or forever hold his
peace."

Reverend Maryland paused. He looked out
over the congregation. Nobody objected so he
went on: "Do you, Eugenia Belle Lazarus, take
this man to love, honor, and cherish for the rest
of your life? Until death do you part?"

Aunt Belle said quietly, solemnly, nervously,
"I do."

"Do you, Monroe Morrison, Junior, take this
woman?" the minister asked.

Robin had looked at him in time to see him
flash his big-toothed grin. Then Monroe said,
"I do." He spoke clearly, loudly.

Robin gave them the rings.

Monroe and Aunt Belle kissed. The next thing
Robin knew, they were racing up the aisle the
way they had come.

Monroe and Aunt Belle stood on the top steps
after everyone had cleared the church. Robin

thought they looked like figures perched on top of a wedding cake. His stomach rumbled. He wished she'd throw the bouquet and get it over with so she could cut the cake.

But Robin soon saw that the newlyweds weren't about to leave. Tex raised a camera he had slung over his shoulder and snapped pictures. After he'd taken twenty or thirty pictures of Aunt Belle and Uncle Monroe, he snapped pictures of Robin and Mr. Lazarus.

Aunt Belle descended a step, stopped, and started swinging the bouquet around and around, like she was on a pitcher's mound or something, Robin thought. When she got through winding up, she flung the flowers out into the crowd.

Robin was standing in the back row, next to his father. Girls and women stood up front, hoping to get a better chance to catch the bouquet. The flowers struck Mr. Lazarus's shoulder, slipped off, and landed in Robin's hands. He grasped it, then lobbed it away like it was a kickball. A girl nearby, hardly older than Robin, caught it. She giggled and ran off to show her mother.

As the newlyweds ran down the steps, they were showered with brown rice. Robin wondered why they were using brown rice. He raced to the curb and opened the car door. And got caught in the shower of rice. Flecks of brown rice landed on his suit. He caught some and examined it. He saw that it wasn't rice at all, but birdseed. Already, wild birds were swooping down out of trees and eating the birdseed on the walkway. Robin kind of wished he'd brought Pollymae. Maybe he could've put her on a leash so she wouldn't fly away. He could've let her peck at the birdseed. But a parakeet at a wedding was a silly idea. Even if she were on a leash.

Robin stood on the curb and watched the car move out into the street. He looked at the JUST MARRIED sign he'd made for the back of it. He'd drawn a crude sketch of a bride and groom beneath the words. And, down near the bottom of the poster, he'd sketched a picture of Pollymae and Watusi.

Tex took another picture of Robin standing on the curb; then the two of them walked back to Robin's house for the reception.

The party had already started when they got there. It wasn't long before the wedding cake disappeared, and all that was left was a plate full of yellow, pink, white, and green crumbs. Robin, never one to say no to cake, had eaten three slices.

"Here, Robin," Aunt Belle said, and offered him a sip of champagne.

When he sipped the champagne, the bubbles tickled his nose. He didn't want to hurt Aunt Belle's feelings, but he didn't like the taste of champagne at all. He thought it tasted like some kind of medicine; like something you'd take for a cold. A real bad cold.

Aunt Belle kissed him, then with a thumb rubbed the lipstick off his cheek. He whispered, "Best wishes." To Monroe, who'd come to stand by his new wife, Robin shook hands and said, "Congratulations, Uncle Monroe."

Robin left them and went to stand near the break in the hedges. He looked around. It seemed like every relative he had and the whole neighborhood was jammed into his backyard. Some couples danced to the music coming from the band, which was playing in a corner of the yard. With so many people there, the yard looked smaller.

He saw Cyndy near the buffet table, sipping punch. She caught his eye and came over to him.

"Let's dance," Cyndy said to Robin. "Let's help your aunt and your new uncle celebrate."

"I don't know how to dance," Robin said, backing off.

Cyndy said, "It's fun. There's nothing to it." She danced alone, demonstrating. "Come on, Robin. You're always saying you can't do something. You really should dance at your own aunt's wedding reception. You were very good as the ring bearer."

"Okay, okay," Robin told her. But he already

knew the steps, even though he'd never danced with a girl. He didn't really want to dance with a girl now, but like bossy Cyndy said, it was a special occasion.

While they danced, he glanced across the yard at his father. The band was playing on four large pieces of plywood they'd put on the lawn. Mr. Lazarus was hunched over the piano, concentrating on his music. The band was really jamming. It didn't sound like a group that was on the verge of breaking up, Robin thought. He hoped Tex was right.

The reception lasted until almost eleven o'clock. Aunt Belle and Uncle Monroe were dancing to the song that Tex had written especially for them. Robin knew that they were getting ready to leave.

Benny and his family were the first to leave. Benny said to Robin, "I must've eaten too much cake. I'll see you when I feel better."

As soon as the song ended, Uncle Monroe went inside and got the suitcases. They had a great distance to travel. Robin hugged and kissed his aunt and his uncle. He saw that his father did the same thing.

Robin sat on the steps and watched his aunt and uncle get into a taxi and go away.

There was one couple still dancing. Robin knew that in a minute or so, they'd leave, too. It was Barry and Terry's parents.

Barry and Terry crossed the yard and came over to Robin. They sat on the steps.

Terry said, "This is some party."

Barry said, "If we'd been at home, we would've been in bed long ago."

Robin smiled, but he didn't feel sleepy at all. The music had stopped. Barry and Terry's parents approached the boys on the steps.

"Hello, Mr. and Mrs. Talbot."

"Hi, Robin," Mr. Talbot said. Mrs. Talbot smiled at him.

They left then. Barry and Terry, still walking side by side, went through the break in the hedges. "See you, Robin," they called from across the yard. They waved, their hands going up simultaneously.

Since there were no more dancers, the band decided to call it a night, too.

After everybody had gone, Robin and his father stood in the yard and looked out over the littered lawn. On the picnic table, lots of mangled paper plates were strewn about. In the center of the table the big cake plate was empty.

"We can clean it up tomorrow," Mr. Lazarus said. "But let's get this paper before the wind blows it away."

They started putting paper plates and cups into a plastic bag. Mr. Lazarus carried it to the garbage can.

"I'm tired," Robin's father said. "How about you?"

"Me, too," he said. But he still wasn't the least bit sleepy. Maybe there'd been too much excitement.

Robin opened the door and they went inside.

Watusi, asleep on the sun porch floor, didn't move a muscle. In her bird cage on the ledge, even Pollymae had gone to sleep.

"The band played great," Robin said when they were in the living room.

"Thanks," Mr. Lazarus said, and smiled. He rubbed his back and stretched and yawned. "That extra practice did us a world of good."

"It was a good wedding, too," Robin said. "I was scared it might rain. Aunt Belle said she was gonna call the whole thing off if it did."

Mr. Lazarus laughed. "She probably never would've. Anyway, Monroe's a nice fellow." He went around and put out the lights. "Listen, off to bed with you. See you in the morning."

"Good night," Robin said, and went upstairs.

Seventeen

THREE weeks after the wedding, the postcards and the letter from Aunt Belle and Uncle Monroe arrived. Robin looked at the colorful, glossy shots of Jamaica and said, "They're already home, and we're just getting their cards."

"They must've gotten mixed up in the mail," Mr. Lazarus said.

" 'Having a wonderful time. Miss you. Love you,' " Robin read the postcards to his father.

"She sent you little messages, at least," Mr. Lazarus said. "All I've got is this fold-out card with a lot of different shots of Jamaica." Mr. Lazarus held the card up. He laughed.

"She wrote us both a letter," Robin told him. They were in the living room, Watusi asleep on top of the TV. He had given up the sun porch floor on the night of the reception. The top of the TV was his new sleeping place.

Robin glanced over at Watusi and then tore the letter open. He read it out loud.

" '. . . this place is wonderful. I think I'm a little old to be a beach bum, but I guess that's what I am. Monroe and I have twelve days here, then it's home again.' "

She'd signed the letter, "Love, Belle and Monroe."

"They've been back a good little while. They've already been house hunting," Robin said.

"Not only that," Mr. Lazarus said. "I think they've found one. Their new address is on the pad by the telephone."

Robin folded the letter and slipped it back into its envelope. He took it to his room, leaving Mr. Lazarus to scratch a few notes on a sheet of music manuscript paper. Mr. Lazarus was getting ready to leave on another trip.

When Mr. Lazarus came upstairs to get ready for his trip, Robin said, "I guess we're still moving. I guess I ought to pack some things, throw some things away." He looked at his father in the doorway.

"There's no getting around it," Mr. Lazarus said. He leaned against the doorjamb. "Well, I guess I'd better get packed." He didn't move. He glanced at the top of Robin's bureau. "Maybe you could throw the night-light out." He left then.

"What time are you leaving?" Robin called across the hall to his father.

"Four-thirty, five o'clock."

"You're going earlier than you used to."

"It's a longer drive this time," Mr. Lazarus said.

Robin lay on his bed and listened as his father threw things into a bag. He heard drawers being opened and closed; the closet door creaking shut; his father taking long strides around the room.

Presently, his father emerged from the bedroom, the small bag in his hand. He stood in the doorway to Robin's room, a serious look on his face. He said, "You be good, Robin."

Robin hated for his father to say that. But it was the one thing Mr. Lazarus could be counted on to say: "Be good, Robin."

He raised himself up on one elbow and looked at his father. He was going to ask him once again if he could come along, but someone rapped on the screen door.

"That must be Isola," Mr. Lazarus said, and went downstairs.

Mr. Lazarus hollered upstairs, "I'm leaving. Robin, be good."

Robin heard the van on the street, its tires squealing, Raimi playing with the horn.

A little while later, he went to the closet and got his battered kickball. He hugged it to his chest and went downstairs.

He spoke to Isola as he went through the living room, but she didn't take her eyes off the TV screen when she murmured back, "Hi." She was watching a hospital show. Robin hurried out of the room. The show'd made him think of his mother, how much he missed her. How she'd died in a hospital.

He went through the dining room and to the sun porch. He glanced at Pollymae but didn't feel like trying to teach her any words today. She'd just have to always sing, Robin thought. He unlatched the screen door and went out to sit on the steps.

Robin held the kickball on his lap, his elbow on the ball. He fidgeted, and the ball rolled off his lap and down the walk toward the street. It didn't go quite to the street. Instead it veered toward the hedges and lodged under them.

Robin was too tired to go after it. He got up and went inside. Isola was still watching TV, but she was also talking on the phone. The hospital show had gone off and a talk show was on. Isola hastily completed the conversation when Robin came into the room.

Turning to face Robin, she said, "I suppose I ought to do something about supper."

"I'm not all that hungry," he said. "Besides,

it's too hot to eat. I'll just have an ice cream cone if I get hungry later.''

But Isola wasn't listening. She had already turned her attention back to the TV. Robin slumped down into the chair. His arms dangled over the sides, his feet spread. How can not doing anything make you so tired? he wondered.

Isola was shaking him. He flung her hands aside. She said, "Listen, Robin, you better go to bed.'' She looked at her watch. "It's a little after nine. What time do you go to bed?''

Robin mumbled something and turned over.

"Robin. Robin, come on, get to bed.''

She finally got him up. He stood, stretched, and yawned. "Good night,'' he said, and started for the stairs. He was still a bit groggy and had to hang on to the banister for support.

By the time he got undressed and into bed, he was no longer sleepy. His room door was open because of the heat. From downstairs he heard Isola switching channels. To him it sounded like she did it every five seconds. Even if he wanted to, he couldn't sleep. He got up and looked at the books in his bookcase. He'd already read them all.

He went to the bureau and reached for the night-light. He palmed it. He leaned down and plugged it in, then went and flicked off the overhead light.

As he climbed into bed, he heard his door creak open wider. Light from the hallway spilled into the room. Watusi had come in and climbed up onto the foot of the bed.

Watusi curled into a ball and went to sleep on the foot of the bed. But Robin still couldn't go back to sleep. Maybe, he thought, I should pack something. He was about to get up and get dressed again, but he heard a knock on the downstairs door. He raised himself up on an elbow and listened. He hoped with all his might that it was his father. Robin heard the door being opened but realized it wasn't his father. His father would've used his key.

From downstairs he heard voices but couldn't make out what was being said. He heard the door open and close again. Then, silence. There wasn't even the sound of the TV.

Robin threw back the covers and got up. He hurried across the hall to his father's bedroom. Leaving the light off, he crept to the window. He pushed the curtains aside and looked out. What he saw was a white car from the Wilkinsburg jitney stand parked in front of the house. He recognized it because he'd often gone past the stand on his way to school. And it was the same car that'd come for his father when his father's car was being repaired.

There was something else that worried him more than anything else. He blinked, making sure that his eyes weren't deceiving him. But it was undoubtedly Isola Humpheries getting into the car on the passenger side. She had a purse slung over her shoulder. Robin turned away from the window.

"She's gone," he whispered to the darkness. He heard the car backfire as it roared away.

Back in his own room, he sat on the bed in the almost darkened room, Watusi at his side. He stroked Watusi's fur. "We've never been in the house alone in the middle of the night," he said to Watusi.

Watusi mewed.

Robin got up and turned on the overhead light. He left the night-light plugged in, too. Without anyone touching it, walking on it, the weak floorboard outside his door creaked like a cherry bomb.

Eighteen

Robin lay back on the bed. But he knew he'd never be able to go to sleep now, not that he was scared. But he did get out of bed and put his clothes on. This is just another time I've been left behind, he thought.

He went out into the hallway. He walked close to the wall, making sure he'd avoid stepping on the creaky floorboard. Hearing it once was enough for one night. The big house seemed larger somehow. He sometimes had to stay alone in the afternoon when he got out of school, until his father came home from his own school. But that was nothing like being alone in the middle of the night.

Robin and Watusi went downstairs. In the

kitchen, he fixed a saucer of milk for Watusi and poured the rest — about a half cup — into a glass for himself.

After he'd finished his milk, he turned on the TV. On one channel was an old horror movie, *Curse of the Undead.* When its eerie music started, Robin switched channels.

This channel, noted for its telecasts of old situation comedies, was showing a war movie. The noises were just as scary as the horror movie on the other channel. He got up and flicked off the set.

He went to the sun porch and peeped in on Pollymae. She was sleeping on her perch like a statue of a bird — very still. He went back to the sofa. "Come on, Watusi. Let's go." But Watusi was already curled up on top of the TV, sound asleep.

Robin crept upstairs again, softly, so he wouldn't wake Pollymae and Watusi. He was still wide awake. The overhead light made the room seem more stifling than it actually was, but he didn't want to turn it off and lie in the dark.

He padded to his dresser and toyed with the things there: bubble gum cards, stickers he'd collected over the years, his comb and brush set, a small picture of Aunt Belle, toy cars he hadn't played with in ages. His fingers came to rest on the letter from Aunt Belle. He didn't read it. What he did was study his aunt's familiar handwriting. It was so large, the few words of his name and address almost covered the entire front of the envelope. He put the letter down and sat on his bed.

He thought: Maybe I'll call Aunt Belle. But in the end, he decided to go to Wheeling to see her. It wasn't so far. He got up, crossed the room, and pulled open the closet door.

On the top shelf, there was a book bag Aunt Belle'd given him last September. It was very roomy. He took it down and carried it to the bed. It was empty. He'd almost never used it for carrying schoolbooks.

He went to the closet again and found a leftover baby blanket. He folded it and put it into the bottom of the book bag. He'd need it to cover Watusi if the bus got cold.

At his bureau he pulled open drawers and took clothing he might need for a short stay. He wanted to see Aunt Belle again, see her after her trip. Even see Uncle Monroe again, too. Anyway, Aunt Belle would never in a million years go off in the middle of the night and leave him all alone.

The bag was full, bulging. He lifted it. It was too heavy, too full. He removed some of the clothing and zipped the bag shut. He sat on the bed again, unsure of his next move.

They had two telephones. A white wall phone

in the kitchen and a red extension in his father's bedroom. He went across the hall and looked up the number for the Greyhound bus station.

"How much is a one-way ticket to Wheeling, West Virginia?" he asked when he'd gotten through to the bus station. He waited. Coming home wouldn't be a problem, he decided. His father would come for him. Maybe Aunt Belle and Uncle Monroe would bring him back. He scribbled numbers on the pad next to the telephone. "Thank you." He hung up the phone, tore off the page he'd written on, and put it into his pocket.

It hadn't been expensive at all, he thought, when he'd gone back into his own room.

On top of the bureau was a bear bank that his mother had given him when he was a baby. He opened the bank and poured the money out onto the bed. There were some bills, but it was mostly coins. Some of it, he knew, probably had been placed there by his mother long ago. It was to be saved for his college education, and he hardly ever touched it. Now he needed it.

Robin counted out the amount he'd need to get to his destination. He also took a bit extra in case he wanted a snack or something.

It made his pockets bulge when he stuffed the money into them, but he didn't care. He swung the book bag up on his shoulder and started out. At his room door, he switched off the overhead light. He looked around to see if he'd forgotten anything.

Out in the hallway he forgot the weak floor-board and stepped smack-dab in the middle of it. A sound like a gunshot reverberated throughout the silent house. Watusi jumped off the bed and ran to the stairs. He stopped and gazed up at Robin.

His heart pounding, Robin clutched his book bag and slowly descended the stairs.

Out on the sun porch, he stopped to say good-bye to Pollymae. He looked into the cage. She was sitting on the perch. Robin thought she looked sad. She wasn't singing. He was a little worried that he hadn't taught her how to talk. But there'd be time for that later.

He had his hand on the doorknob, ready to open it. He looked down. Watusi was rubbing against his leg. Robin wasn't ready to go yet. He had plenty of time to get to the bus. Besides, he was hungry. All he'd had after school was the milk he'd drunk after Isola left. Isola didn't believe in feeding anybody.

Robin pulled the book bag off his shoulder and set it on a chair in the kitchen. There was still a little room in the bag since he'd taken some things out of it. He made two peanut butter and jelly sandwiches, ate one, and wrapped the other and put it into a brown bag for later. His father had baked chocolate chip cookies a few nights earlier. Robin took a handful and put them into the bag.

From the pantry, he got a can of cat food for Watusi. It had a pop top, so he wouldn't need a can opener. He put a small bowl into the book bag. With his lunch and Watusi's the book bag was jam-packed again. He and Watusi moved toward the back door. It was already unlatched; Robin pulled it open.

In her cage on the ledge, Pollymae squawked.

Hold it! Robin thought. You can't leave Pollymae, either. His heart pounded as he realized he'd almost gone out and left her and locked the door. He hadn't taken the keys.

He closed the door and looked at Pollymae. She turned her head to the side and gazed back at Robin.

In the kitchen again he took the book bag off and set it on a chair. He raced upstairs, taking them two at a time. It was getting late now, and he didn't want to miss his bus.

Upstairs in the closet in the room that had been Aunt Belle's, Robin found a small box. His mother had kept all kinds of boxes. The top shelf was piled high with them. She'd used them for packing gifts. She'd said that boxes were expensive and there were never any good ones around when you needed a small one. Sometimes, he remembered, she'd bought Christmas boxes out of season, when they cost less.

However she came by them, she kept them. Robin picked one about six inches by six inches. It was just the size he needed.

Downstairs again, he cut air holes in the box and unfastened the paper clip on Pollymae's cage. He took her out and gently set her in the box. He set the box on the table until he got ready to leave.

He swung the book bag up on his shoulder. Then he checked the key rack on the kitchen wall. He wanted to make sure he could get back in if he had to.

On the rack there were keys to the piano, a key to his father's car, even a key to his mother's jewelry box, but no house key.

He realized Isola must've taken it so she could get back in again without waking him. Maybe he wouldn't need a key. Especially if he got to Aunt Belle's all right. He picked up his things and the box with Pollymae in it, and with Watusi at his heels, they went out.

On the top step, he stopped. The door swung shut. The lock clicked. He was locked out. They could not get back in again. There was nothing to do except go to Wheeling.

It was cooler outside, cloudy, too. Robin was glad he'd decided to wear a long-sleeved sweat-shirt. Even so, he still felt a bit chilly. Damp weather always made him cold.

Two and a half blocks from his house, he

could get the 71 D Hamilton to town. He walked toward the bus stop; Watusi loped along at his heels. In the box, Pollymae didn't make a sound.

The bus was already approaching the corner when they got to the bus stop. The bus halted in front of Robin. He picked Watusi up and climbed aboard. The bus was almost empty. He'd ridden it to town lots of times with his mother, so long ago. Shifting Watusi to his right arm, he dug into his pocket for fifty-five cents.

"Son," the bus driver said, "I can't let you bring that cat aboard without it being in some kind of container. He might get loose and scratch some of the other passengers."

Robin looked around the bus. There were two passengers, both of them sitting in the back. "He won't get loose," Robin said, still fumbling for bus fare.

"You never can tell," the driver said.

"I've got to get downtown. My cat is all right. He hasn't got fleas or anything like that, either."

The driver pushed back his cap and scratched his head. "It's the rules, kid."

They were silent for a moment. A moment that to Robin seemed like an hour. The driver looked at his watch. Robin rubbed his face and hugged Watusi closer to his chest. He turned slowly and climbed down off the bus. In all this time, in the box almost squashed under his arm, Pollymae had not said a word.

Robin didn't know what to do or where to go. But anything, even wandering the streets, was better than staying alone in a big, empty house. He started walking away in the opposite direction of his house. Watusi was still in his arms.

Out in the night, rain-swollen clouds collected in the east; the wind rose. Robin walked on, oblivious to the weight of the book bag and the squirming cat and the unwieldy box with Pollymae.

Several blocks later, Robin put Watusi down. That lightened his load quite a bit. Like a vagabond, Robin moved through the streets, the coins jingling in his pockets.

He still hadn't decided where to go. The Greyhound bus station was all the way downtown. He and Watusi could never walk that distance. He thought of all the communities he'd have to go through: Homewood, East Liberty, Bloomfield, Lawrenceville. No, even if he hadn't brought his pets or the book bag, he still couldn't walk that far.

They hadn't gone much farther when the rain came. It was hardly more than a drizzle at first; then the sky seemed to crack open. They sought shelter under the awning of a store, but the windblown rain soon drenched them. Robin's sweatshirt, soaked through, stretched and hung off his shoulders.

Still standing under the awning, he remembered that there was an old abandoned building about a block or a block and a half away. He'd passed it on the way to school. He picked up Watusi, gripped Pollymae's box carefully, and raced for the building.

Robin hadn't been near the building in a long time. He noticed it was fenced in with plywood, and there were machines inside the fence that were to be used to tear the building down.

It was his only chance for shelter. The rain kept falling harder and colder.

At the fence, he took the book bag off his shoulder and tossed it over. He tucked the box with Pollymae inside under his sodden sweatshirt and grabbed the top of the fence, pulling himself over. It was a good thing he had worn gym shoes. They had traction and his feet didn't slip on the wet plywood. Watusi saw what Robin was doing and easily scurried over the fence.

Once they were inside the building, the rain fell faster. Big silver droplets drummed on the windows, washing the panes almost crystal clear. He felt safe, protected inside the building. When the rain stopped, they could go on their way.

Cold and wet, Robin hugged himself to keep from shivering. Watusi shook water from his fur. It splattered everywhere, including onto Robin. "Watusi! Get back! Don't shake your water on me," he scolded. "I'm already freezing."

Watusi moved over into a corner and lay down on a pile of old newspapers. "That's better," Robin said. "Sometimes I wish I had a dog. They always obey."

Watusi stared at Robin, yawned, and turned over.

Robin took the lid off the box. Pollymae hopped around in the box but didn't fly out. Robin had set it on the floor. He left it there and unpacked some of the things, among them the crib-sized baby blanket. He spread news-papers he'd found on the floor, then opened the blanket out on top of them. He sat on the blanket, facing the door. He wanted to be able to see out, see when it'd stop raining.

He fished into the book bag again and took out the peanut butter and jelly sandwich. He took it out of the bag, peeled off the wrapper, and started eating.

Sniffing, Watusi got up and moved to the blanket. He licked the piece of waxed paper Robin had tossed aside. "Okay, I'll feed you, too."

Holding the sandwich in one hand, he got the can of cat food out of the book bag. He held the sandwich in his mouth and popped the top on the can. He shook the cat food out into the little blue plastic bowl he'd brought along. As soon as he set it in front of Watusi, the cat started eating. "Eat slow," Robin said, rubbing Watusi's back. "I forgot to bring a Thermos of water. We wouldn't've needed it if we could've got on that Greyhound and gone to Aunt Belle's." He bit off his sandwich again. Chewing, he slapped his forehead. "I forgot birdseed." He tore the crusts from around the remainder of his sandwich and crumbled them on top of the paper bag for Pollymae. She ate them right away. I hope she likes chocolate chip cookies, too, Robin thought.

While the three of them ate, the rain fell harder than ever. It was coming down so hard, Robin could hear the cars sloshing along the street. The rain sprayed just like a dam had burst.

He finished his sandwich and went to the door to look out. So much rain poured in under the door that he had to use some of the newspapers to fill the space between the door and the floor. "No wonder they're tearing this building down," he said.

Robin went back to the blanket and lay down, listening to the rain. It beat down faster. He did not feel sleepy at all. He thought that he could rest a bit, and by the time the rain stopped, he could go home again. Maybe Isola would've returned with the key.

But the sound of rain drumming on the glass

128

front of the building soothed him and lulled him to sleep.

He did not awaken until early the next morning. Maybe he would've slept longer, but strange clanging, roaring sounds woke him and made him wonder where he was.

Nineteen

FOR a moment he thought it was the refrigerator cranking up; then he remembered what had happened last night: Isola leaving, how he'd then left for Aunt Belle's, then the cold, heavy rain. He thought about how he and Watusi and Pollymae had sought shelter in the dilapidated building. How he'd slept through the night.

Robin looked out of the plate-glass door. Through the streaked glass, he saw the machines moving closer to the building, like steel dragons ready to pounce on it.

He rubbed his eyes again. He looked out of the glass door. People didn't work on weekends. Although he'd seen the machinery, he thought they'd wait for Monday morning.

Robin had to get out. He turned. Pollymae had flown up out of reach. "Pollymae! Get down!" Robin shouted.

The machines continued to move. One of them had a base that swiveled around. It was the machine with a great steel ball attached to a cable. The machine swiveled and the ball swung around and struck the building. The building trembled. Robin covered his face to protect it from flying glass.

Robin glanced at the rafter. Pollymae was still up there, walking from one end to the other. Robin went to her, but he couldn't reach her.

The ball kept on swinging. Portions of the building began to crumble away as if its bricks were as brittle as the shell on a hard-cooked egg.

Inside there was a crunch as large chunks of Sheetrock broke away from the walls and fell off. Dust sifted down and sprinkled Robin and Watusi and Pollymae with a fine white powder. Pollymae flew higher, up to another window ledge. Robin's black hair turned gray with dust. Watusi shook himself and streaked out of the corner, then burrowed under the blanket. The ball struck again. A board at least six feet by eight inches tumbled down. Still under the blanket, Watusi burrowed to the opposite end of it and scurried out into a far corner.

"Watusi!" Robin yelled. "Get back! We've

got to get out of here!'' Robin started cramming things back into the book bag. He rolled up the blanket. He sat down and started stuffing the blanket into the book bag. Before he could get it crammed in, a four-by-eight plank crashed across his legs, pinning him down.

"OWWWWW!" he screamed.

Watusi took a tentative step out of the corner, toward Robin.

Outside, the machine with a great hinged jaw scooped up a pile of debris, swung around, and spat it onto the bed of a truck.

Robin could only lie there and watch. Pain shot through his left leg from hip to toe. He couldn't move his left leg at all. "Watusi, come here, boy!" It was getting dustier in the building. Robin's face was wet and streaked with plaster dust.

Watusi had gone to huddle in the doorway to an inner office. He peeped around at Robin.

"Get outside. Make them stop. There's got to be a way for you to get out. Scat! Shoo! You're smaller than I am. And there've got to be holes in the walls now." He could feel cool fresh air. He filled his lungs. He looked at Watusi. Watusi hadn't moved. "Go on!" shouted Robin.

Watusi narrowed his eyes, then got up and walked up and down along the wall, looking for a way out. But there was none.

Robin looked around desperately for a brick or a bottle — something, anything — he could throw to try to break the glass. If he could break the glass, he could get the workmen's attention. Maybe.

Then he spied a piece of broken brick. It was almost within arm's reach. He couldn't move because of his injured leg, but he stretched his arm as far as possible. His shoulder ached from the strain. Then he was able to close his fingers around the chunk of brick. He slid it as close as he could and picked it up.

He raised the brick. "Help! Help!" he yelled as he got ready to throw it. What if he couldn't break the glass? What would happen to him? What would happen to Pollymae and Watusi? The parakeet hadn't made a sound, hadn't moved from the top of the window sash.

I should've left them at home, Robin thought. At least they would've been safe. At least they wouldn't all be trapped inside this building.

He gripped the chunk of brick as hard as he could. It felt chalky, brittle in his hand. Maybe it was too old to do anything to the glass. But he had to try. He threw the brick as hard as he could.

It wasn't hard enough. The brick was too old. It glanced off the glass, fell, and shattered. It left a smear of chalklike red dust on the glass.

Then the ball struck the building again. Robin heard a roar like a clap of thunder, then the building swayed and rocked on its foundations.

The dust particles in Robin's eyes felt as big as bricks.

Outside, the machines creaked, the ball swung around, and struck again. The sound was a lot louder now. Robin looked up. He saw that the ball had done a lot of damage to the building. The roof was almost gone. He could see patches of sky.

"If only they'd take a break," he heard himself say. His voice sounded like a stranger's. Pieces of the building continued to fall even when the ball wasn't hitting it. He shouted again, but they still did not hear.

Robin searched around for something else to throw. Pollymae flew off the window sash, then back again. "Can't you find a hole to fly through?" Robin said. But all Pollymae did was circle the room again.

Looking around he saw that a corner of the window over to the right had broken. It was a hole just the size a cat could crawl through, or a bird fly through. He thought: If I can make Watusi go through it . . .

"Watusi, go for the window!" he shouted.

The tortoiseshell cat had been standing in a corner, stretching. Watusi looked at Robin and blinked. He stretched. "Watusi!" Robin pointed a trembling brown finger to the window. Watusi sat down.

Not far from where Robin lay was a piece of soggy newspaper. Robin grabbed it and balled it tight. He threw it at Watusi.

Watusi arched his back and hissed. He hopped up on the narrow windowsill. He sniffed around until he felt cool air blowing through the broken glass. He crept closer to the hole. He stuck his head through, then climbed outside onto the ledge.

"Help! Help!" Robin yelled, as Watusi left. Outside, tail in the air, Watusi trotted over to the men who were sitting in the machines. He jumped into one of the machines.

When Watusi was aboard, he clawed at the man's pants. The man stuck his leg out of the machine and shook it, trying to dislodge Watusi. But the cat wouldn't let go. If anything, Watusi clung tighter, sinking his claws through the khaki fabric of the workman's trousers.

The man hopped out of the machine with Watusi still clinging to him. The man danced around and around, trying to get Watusi to let go.

"Help!" Robin called, hoping to be heard now that the noise wasn't so loud. They can't start up that machine again, he thought.

Outside, others had gathered around the dancing man. They were laughing.

135

Suddenly Watusi let go of the man's trousers and raced toward the door.

On hindpaws, Watusi peered into the building and pressed his head against the glass.

Another man picked up a chunk of wood and tossed it at Watusi, but Watusi wouldn't leave. The man who'd been attached to Watusi's claws frowned. He watched Watusi for a moment, then walked toward the window. He peered inside.

He yelled something that Robin didn't hear, then held up his hand.

Robin looked up. "Help!" he cried. But the man's face had already disappeared from the window. Gently, the man lifted Watusi away from the door, opened it, and still carrying the cat went inside the building.

Twenty

"DON'T move him," the man bending over Robin shouted. He wiped Robin's face with a red handkerchief. Watusi leaned on the man's knee; his forepaws gripped the man's trousers. "Take it easy, little fella," the man soothed Robin. "We sent for an ambulance."

Already, Robin could hear the screams of sirens in the early-morning streets.

One of the men said, "You know, Ralph, I think that cat likes you." They all laughed.

Robin drifted in and out of consciousness. He said, "Did my bird fly away?"

"Nope," Ralph said. "Paul, here, caught him."

Paul came over and kneeled next to Robin so he could see the parakeet.

137

Robin raised himself up and saw that Pollymae was all right.

"How did you get in here?" Ralph asked Robin.

"I shinnied over the fence. I had to. I didn't want Pollymae and Watusi to get wet. The door wasn't locked. It was too far to go back home." Robin's words had come out in a rush, jumbled together.

Ralph and Paul exchanged looks. Ralph said, "It started raining 'round ten, ten-thirty last night."

"That's a long time," Paul said.

"I was scared Pollymae and Watusi would catch colds," Robin told them.

Ralph patted Robin's shoulder. "It's all right."

They didn't get a chance to say more. Two attendants pushing a gurney slogged through the mud. They went into the building. Expertly they lifted Robin off the concrete floor and placed him on the gurney. They strapped him onto it. They wheeled the gurney back outside to the ambulance.

With its siren screaming and tires squealing, the ambulance whisked Robin through the almost-deserted streets. The ambulance didn't stop until it had reached the emergency entrance of the community hospital.

Twenty-one

ROBIN woke up. Mr. Lazarus was unwrapping roses he'd brought and putting them into the water pitcher on the night table.

"Daddy?" Robin said, sounding hoarse and far away.

Mr. Lazarus whirled around. "Oh, you're awake."

"I didn't mean to cause so much trouble. Isola left me, and I didn't want to stay alone anymore. Besides, I wanted to see Aunt Belle and Uncle Monroe again." Robin's words came out in a rush.

"It's all right, son," Robin's father said. He rubbed Robin's forehead. "Everything's all right." He smiled. "Do you feel like having company?"

Robin nodded. Mr. Lazarus went to the door and opened it.

Cyndy and Benny entered first. They were carrying an outsized envelope, Cyndy on one end and Benny on the other. They held it as if it weighed a ton. The rest of the kickball team followed them into the room. They took a giant card out of the giant envelope and put it on the bed in front of Robin.

"Wow!" Robin said. "That's a big card." He read the giant "Get Well" on the card and all the signatures. "Thanks."

Barry and Terry began playing with Benny's kickball. They lobbed it back and forth.

"It's our regular Saturday game," Barry and Terry said together. One twin stood on each side of the bed. They tossed the ball across the bed and back again. Robin lay back, smiling. Roy Butler, Bobby Knuckles, and Cyndy laughed.

With a finger across his lips, Mr. Lazarus said, "Shhhh!"

The gang went right on playing, right on giggling.

After a while, a nurse stuck her head around the door. "Kids! Kids! We can hear you all the way down the hall. Let's keep it down. I don't want to have to ask you to leave!"

After she went away, they were quieter. But to make sure they stayed that way, Mr. Lazarus took their kickball and put it on the windowsill until they got ready to leave.

Mr. Lazarus went over to the bed. He took a felt-tipped pen out of his jacket pocket and, with a flourish, autographed the cast on his son's leg. "Me, too," cried Cyndy. She took the pen and signed her name. Then they all wanted to sign. Soon there were so many signatures on the cast, there was hardly a bare space to be seen.

Later, when the nurse brought Robin's medicine, she autographed the cast, too. And so did the teenage girl from food services who brought Robin's lunch tray.

Mr. Lazarus lifted the silver dome off the plate of steaming food. He said, "Looks good, son." To the kickball team he said, "We'd better get ready to leave."

"Aw, Mr. Lazarus," Barry and Terry said.

Bobby Knuckles and Roy Butler said, "You've even got vanilla ice cream."

Robin smiled and said, "Roy, you and Bobby are beginning to sound like Barry and Terry."

They all laughed, then shook hands with Robin. They followed Mr. Lazarus out into the corridor.

That afternoon, Uncle Monroe and Aunt Belle stopped by. When Robin saw them, he wondered if there were any more stuffed animals and potted plants in the gift shop.

Uncle Monroe carried the potted plants to the windowsill and set them down. Robin didn't know the names of the flowers in them, but he saw that there was a clown-head pot, a brown-bear pot, a pot shaped like a kickball, and a bright green pot that was just square.

Aunt Belle dumped the stuffed animals on the foot of the bed. His aunt and uncle had visited him earlier, or he'd dreamed they were there. However it was, he was still glad to see them. Again.

"I'm so glad you're all right," Aunt Belle said as she hugged and kissed him. When she'd finished, Uncle Monroe grinned his big-toothed grin and shook hands with his new nephew.

Robin had already explained to his father what had happened and didn't want to go into it again.

He needn't have worried. Aunt Belle, sitting down in the big plastic overstuffed chair near the bed, began to talk immediately. "I'm so glad you had my phone number and address on you. When the hospital called me, I called Charles first thing before Monroe and I started the drive here. It's a good thing he still lets me know about the itinerary of the band. I don't know what would've happened. I tried your house, too, and Isola answered. . . ."

142

Then he drifted off to sleep again.

A little while later, Robin awakened again. When he looked up, he saw his father sitting by the bed. Mr. Lazarus was leafing through a magazine.

"Daddy," Robin said, "where's Pollymae and Watusi?"

"They're all right. Don't worry, son." His father stood by the bed.

Reassured, Robin went to sleep again.

When he woke up later, his aunt and uncle had left. He turned to look at the flowers on the windowsill. His mother would've loved them. And she would've made him remember to water them every other day or so, and till the soil in their pots every so often. He stared at the grinning clown-face pot again. The clown had one eye closed and a big gap between its teeth.

It was tedious after a while, to lie there and do nothing. He wished he had a clock in the room, or a wristwatch. He could at least watch time pass. He lay in bed anxiously waiting for his father to come and take him home.

He had been in the hospital long enough. Where was his father?

Using the remote control, he turned on the TV. The TV was suspended from the ceiling and set at just the angle to watch while lying down. He pressed the buttons, flicking from channel to channel, but he couldn't find anything he wanted to watch. He flicked the set off again and put the remote control unit back on the night table. He stared at the ceiling. All he did was think about going home. He wanted to go home in the worst way, although he wasn't sure where home was anymore.

The next day, he was still bored and wondering what to do to pass the time, when he turned over and stared out into the hallway. Maybe, he thought, he'd watch people moving along the corridor.

At first a steady stream of nurses and blue-clad doctors making their rounds were the only people he saw.

Robin craned his neck and tried to see farther down the corridor. He realized it was visiting hours. But he knew it was too early for someone to visit him. Yesterday he had all his visitors in the afternoon. He continued looking out into the hallway, hoping someone would stop by his room. He saw lots of people in regular street clothes walking slowly up and down the corridor looking for room numbers.

He had turned his head away from the door and was staring at the ceiling when out of the corner of his eye he saw that someone *had* stopped at his room. Before he turned his head and looked squarely at his visitor, he hoped it'd be his father coming to take him home.

The figure in the doorway was wearing a blue striped shirt and navy blue slacks. Under one arm, he carried a white gift box. In the other was a big cowboy hat. This visitor wasn't Robin's father, but he was just as welcome.

Going into the room, Tex fanned Robin with the cowboy hat. "Hello, there," he said.

Robin grinned and said, "Hi, Tex."

Tex tossed the cowboy hat onto the night table. "Here you go," he said as he handed Robin the gift-wrapped package he'd brought.

Wondering what it could be, Robin tore at the wrapping paper. He got the package open.

"It's a keyboard instrument," Robin said. He opened the box and removed the gift.

"I put some batteries in," Tex told him. "Go on, play something."

Robin pushed the ON button and played a few licks.

"Sounds like you've been practicing on your father's piano," Tex said.

"Sometimes."

Of course, Tex autographed Robin's cast. He sketched a guitar onto the plaster and wrote his name inside.

After Tex had left, Robin played the keyboard. It was a good thing he could adjust the volume on it, like a radio. He wouldn't have to worry about disturbing the other patients.

He was glad Tex had brought him a portable keyboard. Now he could make music sometimes instead of lying there and changing channels on the TV. He had something interesting to do until his father came to take him home.

Twenty-two

For the thousandth time, Robin wondered what was keeping his father. With every movement down the corridor, however small, he'd crane his neck to see if it was his father.

Bored, he had turned to stare at the flowers again when Mr. Lazarus burst into the room. "All set?" he asked as he set the suitcase on the floor and placed the bag with Robin's going-home clothes on the foot of the bed.

With both hands Robin gripped his leg with the cast and inched his way to the edge of the bed. Mr. Lazarus came to the bed and helped Robin to the floor.

Just then a nurse came into the room carrying a large box. "Mr. Lazarus," she said, "I found

147

this box. Maybe you can use it for some of these stuffed animals, and fruit, and flowers.''

"Yes. Yes. Thanks," Mr. Lazarus said.

Mr. Lazarus took the box and started packing things into it. First, he cleared the potted plants off the windowsill, then what was left of the basket of fruit from Raimi and Luther. Then he packed Tex's gift, which had come with its own box.

Mr. Lazarus looked up. Robin, wearing navy camper's shorts, was staring at the lilac polo shirt. "Do you need any help getting dressed?" his father asked.

"No," Robin said. He clutched the shirt.

Mr. Lazarus stopped filling the box. Robin could see that it was already jam-packed with things he'd acquired while in the hospital. The head of a great stuffed bear jutted out of the box, staring at him.

Robin looked at the polo shirt. He was wadding up the bottom half of it, even squeezing it.

"Son, what's the matter?"

He had wanted to tell his father how he felt. He didn't stop to try to form the proper words. He said, "I don't want to move. The house where we live is the only home I ever lived in and I want to stay there. I miss my mother. You keep going off to play the piano. I knew I wouldn't see Aunt Belle much. But Isola didn't

148

have to leave me in the middle of the night like that." He started crying then.

Mr. Lazarus took a step forward. He lifted Robin up and held him.

"Pollymae and Watusi were the only ones who didn't go away," Robin said, sniffling.

"It's all right,"Mr. Lazarus said. "Things'll be a lot different now. I'm going to take you on the road sometimes." His father's voice trembled.

Mr. Lazarus put Robin down in the big plastic overstuffed chair and strode around the room.

"You know, I've missed your mother a lot, too. I guess I tried to play music so I wouldn't think. Maybe I wanted to pretend she was still there. I don't know. I was so busy hiding my grief that I just ignored you altogether." Mr. Lazarus stopped pacing and sat on the edge of the bed.

Robin pulled a tissue out of the box on the night table and dabbed his eyes and blew his nose. He realized his father had hugged him for the first time in — well, in a long, long time.

With his hands clasped, Robin sat in the big chair. Mr. Lazarus sat on the edge of the bed. They looked at each other for a long moment.

Then Robin's father said, "Son, we're going to be all right."

"I guess so," Robin said. He saw that he was

still gripping the lilac polo shirt. He stared at it and thought about how his mother had bought it for his birthday, how he had worn it to sing in the choir at the Christmas play. His mother would've wanted him to wear it before he outgrew it. She always used to say, "You're growing so fast. You're almost as tall as I am." He smiled to himself, remembering.

He shook the lilac polo shirt, then slipped it slowly over his head.

"I'm going to take this box down to the car. Be right back," his father said, and lifted the box and went out.

Robin grabbed the big card off the bed and slipped it back into its envelope.

"I'm all set," he said, as his father came back into the room. He tucked all the cards he had received under his arm.

"Can you carry those cards all right?" Mr. Lazarus asked.

"Yes, I guess," Robin answered.

"Come on, then. I have a surprise for you."

Ordinarily, Robin liked surprises. But now he was afraid to ask what the surprise was. His father could've moved them off to a weird apartment while he was in the hospital.

His father did not have to help him into the car. The cast was shaped like a boot and covered half his foot and went up his leg to just below the knee. The doctor had made elevations for his heel and toe.

Robin maneuvered his body into the front seat. When his father had offered to help him, Robin had said, "I have to try to do as much as I can on my own. The nurse says it's part of my therapy."

So Mr. Lazarus got behind the wheel, and when they'd buckled their seat belts, he tooled the car expertly out of the hospital parking lot.

Traffic was light and Mr. Lazarus drove slowly through the streets. It was making Robin edgy. He wanted to know what his father's surprise was, yet he didn't want to know. It might be something bad, he thought. Very bad. His father's leisurely driving was also about to lull him to sleep. He had almost dozed off when he felt the car going downhill. He leaned forward and looked out of the window at the familiar surroundings.

"We didn't move," Robin said as they pulled into their driveway.

Mr. Lazarus didn't say anything until he'd stopped the car and they'd climbed out. He had come around to the passenger side and opened the door for Robin.

Robin stared at the house — his house — for a long, long time. Mr. Lazarus put his hand on Robin's shoulder.

"Did you really think I'd move away like that

151

while you were cooped up in the hospital? This is home. Your mother and I picked this house out together. We thought it was perfect. Close to the schools — mine and yours. We're only a stone's throw from the shopping center.

"But you know, she loved that fireplace. The first nip in the air, she built a fire. And the yard. That was her pride."

Robin looked at his father. Mr. Lazarus grinned. Robin smiled back at his father.

"As long as I have something to say about it, we won't be moving."

"You said you had a surprise. . . ."

They stood silently on the walkway. Robin saw Raimi's van parked at the curb. And Uncle Monroe's car right next to it, almost touching.

Robin heard the screen door open. He turned his head and stared. One by one, they rushed outside: Luther twirling his saxophone strap; Tex, wearing his cowboy hat; Aunt Belle and Uncle Monroe holding hands.

Although Robin had not expected to see his kickball teammates, they raced from around back of the house. When they'd climbed up on the porch with the grown-ups, they all shouted, "Welcome home, Robin!"

Mr. Lazarus gripped Robin's hand. "That's the surprise, son."

When he went into the living room, Robin

could hear Pollymae out on the sun porch singing her head off.

Robin saw that Watusi was exactly where he thought he'd be. The cat was lying on his side on top of the TV, his tail swinging back and forth in front of the screen. He turned his head and blinked at Robin as if Robin had never been away.

Robin went through the dining room and out onto the sun porch. For a few seconds, Pollymae stopped singing and cocked her head to the side, looking at Robin. Robin said, "Hello." Pollymae squawked, then started singing again.

Robin went back into the living room. He eased down onto the sofa. Watusi was still swinging his tail back and forth in front of the TV screen.

His head pressed against the back of the sofa, Robin listened to the sounds of the band members tuning their instruments. There was feedback from the microphone, too.

Out in the kitchen, the refrigerator cranked up, clicked on, and roared to life. Sounds bombarded him from both sides, the cellar on his left, the kitchen on his right.

Robin noticed that the refrigerator didn't sound as loud as it had before. He guessed Aunt Belle had had Uncle Monroe look at it.

The sounds didn't matter. They weren't very

unpleasant at all. Presently, Robin heard a much more soothing sound coming up from the cellar. His friends cheered at the first strains of music as the band members began to play. Carefully, he slid off the sofa and went down to the cellar to join them.

In the cellar, he could still hear the refrigerator. No, he thought, the sounds weren't unpleasant at all. It just made him realize he was home again. Home at last.

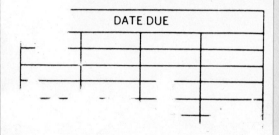

Wilson, Johnniece M.
Robin on his own

DATE DUE		